Be careful what you wish for, you just might get it.

DESTINY OF A COP

Inspired by more than twenty-seven
years as a Phoenix police officer

D1738239

L. D. ZINGG

ISBN-13: 978-1985579996

ISBN-10: 1985579995

First Edition: 2018.01

Edited by Tesz Millan

Cover design and story format by John Ingle

Published by L. D. Zingg, LLC

LDZingg@gmail.com

FaceBook: LD Zingg

Available at Amazon.com

9·25·'28

To Kori

Best Wishes!

Dedication

To my wife, Lois Ann, my daughters, Cydney and Jennifer, and to my son Mark, who was called to his heavenly home while in the prime of his life. And to all who have endured, and those who continue to endure, the sacrifices of life as the family of a law enforcement officer. And to farmers everywhere, whose endless toil of the land produces only what Mother Nature will allow.

Acknowledgments

Thanks to my family and friends for their encouragement and critiques. Their input was invaluable in the development of this story. A special thanks to my daughter, Jennifer Zingg, and to John Ingle, without whose assistance this story would still be stuck somewhere in my mind or in my computer.

Other books in this series

LIARS ALL

THE LIGHT OF TRUTH

WHERE IT ALL BEGAN

Other works by this author

THE POETRY OF LIFE

Children's Books

BARNYARD FRIENDS

A ROBIN INVITED ME TO DINNER

There were times when I felt as if I had no will of my own; like a grain of sand being pushed and pulled by the tide of destiny. Unknowing and unrefined at first, but through trial and error, I was molded into the life I was destined to lead, the job I was destined to do, and the person I was destined to become.

A GRAIN OF SAND

A grain of sand on an endless beach
At the mercy of the tide
No obstacles to face or breach
Just going along for the ride

Unfettered freedom was not to be
It was swallowed up by fate
Taken by the briny sea
No force to man the gate

Bound and blinded evermore
Without a ray of light
A darkened place so far from shore
The dull now polished bright

Formed and shaped by years of toil
Within a confined space
The clam of life released its spoil
A pearl now in its place

L. D. Zingg

PART ONE – DESTINY REVEALED

"By three methods we learn wisdom: First, by reflection, which is the noblest; second, by imitation, which is the easiest, and third, by experience, which is the bitterest." – Confucius

CHAPTER ONE

Northern Iowa

May 1943

The gate flew open and bounced slowly back, coming to rest against the latch, as nine-year-old Luke Canfield bolted through on his way to the barn. A voice in his head urged him to go back and latch the gate. He slowed and glanced quickly around to see where the voice had come from. No one was in sight. He shrugged it off and continued to the barn.

Luke's father had often cautioned him to make sure he latched the gate between the house and the farmyard so Evelyn, his three-year-old sister, and Whiskers, their pet goat, couldn't wander into the yard. The open stock tank was too inviting and dangerous for a child. Normally, he made sure he did. But today wasn't normal. His mission was more important than a swinging gate. Little Roanie was having her first calf, and Luke was determined to be there.

He'd seen other cows give birth, but this one was special. He'd raised her from a runt. Calves too frail to survive without special care were penned in the apple orchard south of the house until they were nursed back to health. It was Luke's responsibility to care for them until they gained proper weight. By the time they were grown they'd become pets. It was a bittersweet achievement. Once they were able they rejoined the herd.

Even at age nine, Luke reconciled himself to that fact of farm life. So it was with Little Roanie, named for her underdeveloped body and mottled orange and white color. She was now fully grown and about to have her first calf.

Since none of the men were available, it was up to Luke to see that his pet cow delivered her baby safely.

His mother and four older sisters were busy cleaning house and preparing the mid-day meal. His father and four of his brothers were in the field. Another day or two and they'd have the corn planted. His other two brothers, Andrew and Henry, were off to war. Two fringed banners with a blue star hung in the front window. They would remain there until the boys came home.

Luke prayed for them every night. He wondered if God ever heard him. He'd never gotten a sign, although he'd asked for one a number of times. Even without a sign, the prayers would continue until his brothers were safely home. Besides, God was probably too busy protecting them and all the other brothers to answer everyone who asked for a sign. He also prayed that his brother, Arnold–four years old when he died of pneumonia–had found someone in Heaven to play with.

He often wondered if dogs went to Heaven. If they did, his brother would have Shep to keep him company. Luke missed that smelly old dog.

With a mighty heave, Luke pushed open one of the large sliding doors and entered the barn. The barn was one of his favorite places. He was familiar with every square inch of the building. He spent nearly as much time there as he did outdoors, especially in the winter. The smell of hay, grain, cattle, and even the manure was always reassuring. It made him feel connected in some way, not only to the land, but to a lifestyle.

Everything he could possibly want was tied to the farm. His family was there. His pets were there–one goat, two dogs, and twenty-eight cats at last count. He'd been born there. His father had delivered him on the kitchen table during a blinding snowstorm. Farming was in his blood. It was the only life he knew, and the only one he wanted to know. He intended to remain a farmer forever.

"Mmmm-bawww!" The plaintive bellow caused the hair on the back of Luke's neck to rise. He hesitated before peering around the corner of the feed bin to see the cause of such a bone-chilling sound.

Little Roanie was lying down, her sides heaving as she strained to deliver her calf. He could see the little black hooves protruding from under the cow's tail. She needed help. He'd seen similar situations many times, but his father or one of his brothers had always been there to take charge. This time it was up to him.

Just as he'd seen his father do, he sat down on the cement floor behind the cow and braced his bare feet against her rump. He grabbed the slippery little hooves and pulled with all his might. Nothing happened. He needed to get a rope and rig up a pulley.

As he frantically searched for the right equipment, a feeling of dread engulfed him, flooding his brain with the realization that his little sister was in trouble. It was as if she was inside his head screaming for help. The feeling overwhelmed him and sent him reeling. He gasped for breath as he staggered to the door and lurched through.

A quick glance to the lawn where he last saw Evy and

Whiskers sent an icy chill rippling down his spine. The gate was ajar and they were nowhere in sight.

He swung his gaze across the yard and east to the windmill with the large cement holding-tank next to it. He spotted Whiskers nearby. Evy must be there too.

Luke ran as fast as he could. His bare feet kicked up little spurts of dust and an occasional pebble as he flew across the yard. Everyone knew the dangers of the open water tank that was kept filled for the cattle and horses. The kids were often cautioned not to play around it.

His heart sank as he neared the tank in time to see Evy's limp body slip silently beneath the surface. Without hesitation, he jumped in where he'd seen her go down. Searching frantically for the submerged little body, he was relieved when her hair brushed against his hand. He grabbed a handful, pulled her to the side of the tank, and hoisted her out of the water.

He didn't see his father coming. He just saw a big hand reach down, jerk Evy up and begin shaking the water out of her, holding her by the ankles and slapping her on the back.

Almost immediately she began to cough up water and cry. Her father swung her upright and hurried her into the house. Tears, blended with mill-water, rolled down Luke's cheeks as he followed closely behind.

Luke's pulse slowed to a more normal rate as a sigh of relief puffed from his lips. He knew he was in trouble, but his father hadn't said anything so maybe he wasn't. He went out on the porch, trying to prepare himself for what his father was going to say. After a few minutes, his father joined him.

"I can't believe you would let your little sister play around the stock tank. I've told you how dangerous it is. Why did you do such a thing?"

The edge in Dan Canfield's voice was something Luke had never before heard. He glanced up to see his father glaring at him. His brow was furrowed like the rows of a plowed field and his mouth tightened into a grimace. The disapproving look and steely tone were frightening. Luke needed to say something, quick.

"We weren't playing around the tank. Honest, Dad," Luke pleaded. "I thought Evy was on the lawn with Whiskers. I was in the barn helping Little Roanie. I don't know how Evy got out. Maybe the gate didn't latch when I ran out. My mind told me Evy was in trouble so I ran and helped her out of the water. I don't know how I knew. I just knew."

Luke hesitated to continue under his father's angry glare, but an emergency situation still needed to be dealt with. "We need to get to the barn. Little Roanie needs help, Dad." The words flew from Luke's mouth.

His father turned and without a word, strode to the barn with Luke hot on his heels.

As they entered the building and rounded the corner of the feed bin, Luke heaved a sigh of relief. He hadn't realized he'd been holding his breath until his lungs ached. He let it out in one big whoosh.

Little Roanie was up and licking the miniature image of herself. The little roan calf struggled to stand, but its wobbly legs wouldn't permit it. A second wave of relief rushed over Luke to see that both the mother cow and her baby were fine, but he was more relieved that his little sister was safe.

He knew he had to come up with an explanation, but he couldn't figure out how to convince his father that he hadn't disobeyed his orders not to play around the stock tank. He couldn't explain the voice in his head, or his sudden knowledge that Evy was in desperate need of help. It was too complicated to even *think* about, let alone *talk* about. He stood silently, waiting. Dan Canfield had never struck any of the kids. One look or a stern word was enough to set them straight.

Luke joined his father on some sacks of grain piled in front of the manger. Each sat quietly. The only sound came from Queenie munching an ear of corn. Luke liked to hear a horse crunch corn off the cob, but this time it barely registered.

Finally, after what seemed like forever, his father turned to him and said, "Tell me how you knew Evy was in trouble if you weren't there." His voice still had an edge to it.

"I don't know," Luke said. "It just came to my mind. I felt scared, *real* scared. I couldn't hardly breathe. I just knew she was in trouble and I ran to help her. I don't know how I knew...I just knew."

His father shifted his gaze back and forth between his son and a tabby cat prowling around the barn, known to always take a circuitous route to a litter of kittens that were stashed in a corner of the haymow.

"I've never known you to lie," Dan Canfield said. "I'm not sure what to make of your explanation. Common sense tells me your story is highly doubtful. But I guess stranger things have happened."

His father rubbed his chin reflectively, then slowly turned to face his son. "I'm proud of you for getting your little sister out of the water. You probably saved her life. But I'm disappointed that you didn't make sure the gate was latched."

Luke fought hard to hold back the tears. Try as he might, they tumbled down his cheeks and splashed onto his bare feet. He hung his head. He didn't want his father to see him cry. Boys weren't supposed to cry–especially farm boys.

"It may not be something you *meant* to do," his father continued in a calm, but stern voice, "but it's something you *neglected* to do, and that can be just as bad."

With head bowed and his throat feeling as if he'd swallowed a mouthful of sand, Luke remained silent as his father placed a calloused, sunbaked hand on his son's shoulder.

"I know you were in a hurry to help the cow give birth, but your first responsibility was to see that the gate was latched. Never skip over something important just because you're anxious about something else. As you see, Little Roanie was able to give birth without our help. Animals have taken care of themselves long before humans were around, and they will continue to do so."

He gave Luke's shoulder a gentle squeeze. "It's the lack of attention to detail, the little things that get people into trouble. Take care of the little things. The big things will often take care of themselves."

His father's voice had softened from the harsh tone a few minutes earlier, but his words still seared Luke's brain like a steak on a griddle. They set a standard for him to live by. Anything less was unacceptable.

If it took him a lifetime, Luke promised himself he would find a way to prove to his father that he was being truthful. He hadn't realized until this very moment how important the truth was, and how devastating it was not to be believed. He wished there was a truth machine that could prove he wasn't lying.

He didn't understand everything that had happened, but deep in Luke's bones, he knew something besides a calf was born that day. A special gift had been revealed. An insight into another person's mind. In one life-changing moment, his destiny was determined. Conceived in chaos, born of desperation, and nourished by situation and circumstance, his new-found ability propelled him on a search for truth, and destined him to become a cop.

L. D. Zingg

PART TWO – THE STRANGER

"An invisible thread connects those who are destined to meet,
regardless of time, place, and circumstance.
The thread may stretch or tangle. But it will never break."
— Ancient Chinese proverb

CHAPTER TWO

Waterloo, Iowa

April 1954

Stalag 17 was playing at the State Theater on that rainy Saturday afternoon. Seventeen-year-old Emily Thurston went to the movies alone. As an only child she was used to going by herself. She was too sensitive and became too emotional during the sad parts. It embarrassed her friends.

She didn't particularly like war shows, but this one was more about conflict of personalities than it was about political differences. She enjoyed witnessing the complicated interaction of people. It fulfilled her emotional needs to see how others had overcome their struggles. Maybe she could find answers to some of her own.

Emily had carried a burden of guilt since the age of eleven when her father crossed the center line and struck another car head-on. He was *dead-drunk* before he was dead. Although traveling alone, he wasn't the only casualty. The wreck also claimed the lives of a mother and father and severely injured two of their six children.

A court awarded the Thurston family holdings to the victim's children. In a few short months, Eleanor Thurston and her daughter, Emily, had gone from being one of the wealthiest families in town to one of the poorest.

Mercy is never shown to the relatives of an offender. But Eleanor never complained. She worked hard to keep up a front. She cautioned her daughter never to let on about their emotional and financial struggles. Eventually, they moved away to start a new life where no one knew their legacy.

Emily never told anyone about her childhood, not even her closest friends. But somehow the family name was still associated with status. The daily paper welcomed them to the area. Only those of prominence were ever awarded that distinction. There was no mention of the accident. All anyone knew about Emily Thurston was that she came from a prominent family.

She cringed every time someone mentioned how fortunate

she was to have been born into wealth. They didn't know about the years of abuse. Or about the times her father came home in a foul mood, reeking of whiskey. Or the times he didn't come home at all. The birthdays missed. The promises broken. The increasing violence. The countless nights she hid under her bed and shook with fear, a pillow pulled tightly over her ears in a futile attempt to drown out his drunken rants. And they didn't know about her attempts to intercede when her mother was beaten, only to end up bruised and battered herself.

The scars on Emily's body had long since healed. But the ones in her mind were still raw. Those were the ones that made her suspicious of promises and mistrustful of men. Her father had promised to always love and care for her mother. He promised his only child he'd always be there for her. But he'd let them both down. Maybe one day, Emily would find someone she could trust, someone who would treat her kindly and never leave, but she wasn't holding out much hope.

The violent years were never discussed. Both women felt guilty, as if it had been their fault. There was obviously something lacking in them that made them targets of abuse. Clinging to that belief was easier than admitting that Luther Thurston loved the bottle more than he loved his wife and daughter.

A counselor said Emily and her mother were victims. He

said it wasn't their fault. Nevertheless, the guilt lingered. She was certain she'd played a role in her father's death; for in those terror stricken moments, alone under her bed, hearing her mother's screams, she prayed he would die.

He always calmed down after a drunken rant. The night of the accident was no different. He was sorry. He promised to quit drinking. He said he'd never meant to hurt anyone. He even got down on his knees to beg forgiveness. But Emily didn't buy it. She'd heard the same speech too many times before.

"I hate you. I wish you were dead," she screamed as her father staggered out the door.

She didn't tell the doctor about wishing and praying her father would die. She couldn't bring herself to speak the words. He would think she was evil. Maybe even put her away in a crazy-house. The thought was overwhelming.

She also felt guilty about the two innocent people in the other car whose deaths left six orphaned children. If she had accepted her father's apology and not wished and prayed so hard that he would die, he and the people in the other car would be alive today. She could have survived the bruises. She didn't mean it when she'd wished him dead.

Her childhood was something Emily tried not to think about. But there were occasions when her efforts proved fruitless.

Today was one of those occasions.

She didn't count on becoming personally involved with the movie. She reminded herself the story wasn't real. But seeing a man beaten for something he didn't do, triggered memories that she'd tried desperately to keep buried.

Emily knew firsthand the stinging sensation of violence. She could feel every impact. But the emotional blows hurt the most. Tears rolled down her cheeks and into the corners of her mouth. Her nose ran. The sniffles grew louder and more frequent. People moved away.

She didn't notice the young man who silently sat down beside her until he handed her a handkerchief. He didn't say a word. He didn't even look her way. He quietly held the piece of cloth in front of her face until she reluctantly accepted it, wiped her eyes and blew her nose.

After the movie, Emily and her benefactor made their way to the lobby. She turned to thank him. At 5'10," she was taller than most boys she knew, but she had to look up to get a good view of this young man with the short brown hair and rugged face.

He wasn't the most handsome man she'd ever met, but he had a warm smile and a nice tan obviously left over from last summer. He wasn't her knight in shining armor either. Definitely not the one she had always envisioned would come riding up on a white horse and save her.

She had longed to be rescued from the nightmare of her childhood, but her hero never came. Now he was here. But instead of romantic shining armor, he was wearing stupid-looking bib-overalls. Pa Kettle wore clothes like that.

Emily stifled a laugh. "Thanks very much for the handkerchief," she said as she dangled the cloth in her hand.

It was an awkward moment. She was unsure what to do with it. She didn't want to hand it back after blowing her nose in it. "I'm sure you don't want it back now." She chuckled at the thought.

"That's OK. You can keep it." He blushed.

He still hadn't looked her in the eyes. He kept his head turned away. She couldn't tell if he was just shy, or if he was "different."

"Is it a long way to your car? It's really pouring out there." His voice was filled with concern.

"I don't have a car," Emily said, bemused by the charitable act as well as at the appearance of the stranger who had come to her aid.

Stranger was a good word for him. He was stranger than anyone she'd ever met. She grinned at the thought, but he didn't seem to notice. "I walked to the theater. I only live a few blocks from here."

"You can't walk home in this storm." He gestured to the rain pouring down. "I'd be happy to give you a lift. My car is right across the street." Concern showed in his big brown eyes when he finally glanced her way.

Ordinarily, she wouldn't have accepted. She didn't trust men. Her mother had encouraged a relationship with Max Gordon, a banker's son who worked as a teller. They went out a few times, but all he talked about was how much money he was going to make and how important he was going to be. Emily wasn't impressed. Her father had been wealthy and important too. He was also an abusive alcoholic who drove drunk and ended up killing himself and two others.

Max still hung around, even after she told him she wasn't interested in a long-term relationship. The saying "familiarity breeds contempt" was coined for her. She grew tired of boys after a few dates. They were all braggarts, concerned only with themselves.

She shuddered whenever Max Gordon's name was mentioned. Her last date with him had been a nightmare. He hadn't taken kindly to being rejected. She tried to put it out of her mind, but every once in a while it crept back in. She never told anyone what he did to her. She couldn't bring herself to say it. Everyone would blame her for "leading him on," as she'd heard people say. She would carry the shame to her grave.

But this young man standing before her was kind enough to offer his handkerchief, and it was raining pretty hard. Besides, how could someone who dressed like Pa Kettle and who was too shy to look her in the eyes be anything but a gentleman? She accepted his offer.

They dashed across the street to his green Ford Sedan. Even though it was raining buckets, the young stranger opened the passenger door and made sure Emily was safely seated before he climbed in.

"I'm Luke Canfield," he said.

He kept his eyes fixed on the road as she directed him to her house.

"I'm Emily Thurston," she replied. "Thanks for rescuing me twice–first the handkerchief and then the rain."

She chuckled, not only to keep the conversation light, but to keep the boy at arms-length. She didn't want him thinking she was a pushover, or that she owed him anything. But he had been considerate and sensitive to her needs. The least she could do was speak kindly to him. She was surprised by how comfortable she felt in his presence.

"Glad I could help." He sounded sincere.

Luke slowly pulled up to her house at 308 South Street. "You better wait a few minutes and let the rain ease up or you're going to get soaked." He glanced briefly in her direction, both hands on the steering wheel.

She had gripped the door handle, prepared to jump out and run for the porch as soon as they came to a stop, but his suggestion made sense. She decided to wait a few minutes.

"Am I keeping you from anything?" She looked full at him.

He glanced her way and grinned. "No, I have time. It's too wet to get in the field, and I don't have to do chores for another hour." His voice was clear, matter of fact.

"What kind of chores?" Emily asked.

"Milk the cows, slop the hogs, and about a million other things," he replied. "But if you came along and helped me I'd get through a lot faster." He was staring straight ahead, his hands clasped tightly around the steering wheel.

Slap a hog? Was he joking? He must be. He turned his head. She noticed a smile. Of course he was joking. His brown eyes lit up when he smiled. She liked that. "I'm afraid I couldn't bring myself to slap a hog. Why would you want to do that anyway?"

He let out a hearty laugh. "Not *slap*. *Slop*. That just means

I have to feed the hogs. We mix water, ground oats, mineral and milk in a big barrel and pour it into a trough. The hogs love it. It puts weight on and gets them to market faster." He sounded enthused.

"Don't you have anyone there to help you?" she asked.

"My brothers have all married and moved away," he said. "My dad and I are the only men left to do the work. My dad is getting up in years, so I do everything I can so he doesn't have to."

He explained everything with a straight face so he's apparently serious about his chores. "Well, I'd better go and let you get to your slapping or slopping." She turned to go.

"How about going to the movies with me next time it rains?" he hurriedly asked. "Rainy days are about the only time I can get away from the farm. No...I don't want to wait that long. How about next Saturday night? I could pick you up."

She wasn't sure what to say. He had obviously lost some of his shyness. He looked full at her with his sparkling brown eyes. If he came back Saturday, she would have time to wash his handkerchief and give it back. That was the least she could do to repay his kindness.

"OK. I'll be ready when you get here." She quickly climbed out and dashed up the walk.

She didn't learn until several dates later that on the

day they met, Luke had left three of his buddies at the theater watching the credits run while he took her home.

Out of a sea of people, a seventeen-year-old city girl and a twenty-year-old farm boy had found each other.

***

There was a full moon, the night he asked her to be his girl. They were out riding in the country as they had so many times since they'd met. The loose gravel roads were a perfect excuse to drive slow and make the evening last.

Luke pulled into the driveway of a cornfield near the family farm. They sat for a few minutes listening to the incessant chirp of crickets and the occasional croak of a bullfrog before he fished into his pocket. He took Emily's hand and slipped a ring on her finger.

She carefully examined it in the moonlight. It was bright blue and made of expandable plastic. Her first thought was that it came from a box of Cracker Jacks. But she had opened many a box of the tasty snacks and had never come across a ring like that.

"Well, how do you like it?" he asked with a grin.

"I think it's lovely," she quipped. "But you shouldn't have spent your hard earned money on such a beautiful ring."

"Oh, that's all right. It actually didn't cost me anything," he replied. "I can't afford a real ring, but this one will let you know how I feel."

He took her hand and held it to his lips. "This is actually a chicken ring."

"A chicken ring?" Emily asked. "Why would chickens wear rings?"

Luke chuckled while trying to explain. "We put a ring on a chicken's leg so we can keep track of the best layers."

Emily turned the ring over and over on her finger before busting out in a laugh. "Are you saying I'm a good layer? Or is it a good lay?"

Luke was caught by surprise. He hadn't considered that aspect of the ring. He needed to think quickly.

"It's just a reminder that I think you're great in everything you do," he said.

He slid out from under the steering wheel and gathered her in his arms.

Emily turned her head and met his lips with an eagerness and a passion far beyond that which she had previously demonstrated.

After a deep and prolonged kiss, she turned her head and nuzzled his ear. "Since we're engaged…We are engaged…aren't we?" she hesitantly asked. "And you are going to marry me?"

"Yes," he quickly replied.

"Well, then, I want you to make love with me," she whispered.

Luke didn't know what to say. He wanted desperately to make love to her. But what if she got pregnant? He wasn't ready for that. He wasn't making enough money to support himself, let alone a wife and child.

His mind was still churning as Emily undid his belt and unzipped his pants. Deftly, she slipped off her panties and straddled his lap. "Raise up," she whispered as she tugged on his trousers.

He raised his body and helped her lower his trousers and shorts. With guidance from her right hand, he slipped into her easily and for a minute, neither moved as the ecstasy of the moment seemed to overwhelm them both. Then, with a low moan, Emily began moving her body back and forth in slow, rhythmic thrusts.

A combination of starbursts and bottle rockets suddenly exploded in Luke's head and ricocheted through every cell in his body.

"No," she yelped as he quickly withdrew and spewed his semen on the floor of the car. "Why did you do that?" she whimpered, clinging tightly to him.

"I'm sorry," he said. "I didn't want you to get pregnant. I'm sorry. I should have waited until I could get some rubbers."

Sobbing quietly, Emily rolled off him and pulled on her panties.

"I'm sorry," he repeated, attempting to console her.

"It's OK," Emily whispered as she embraced him. "But I wouldn't have cared if I did get pregnant."

He pulled up his shorts and trousers and buckled his belt before sliding under the steering wheel. They rode in silence back to her house.

Luke walked Emily to the door and held her tight.

"Next time it's my turn," she said. "So you had better be prepared to last longer."

The porch light cast a glow on Emily's face that enhanced her loving smile. "I can hardly wait until next time," she said softly, "so don't wait until it rains before you show up again. You will show up again, won't you?" she teased.

"Damn, you are beautiful," Luke said. He leaned in to kiss her. "I'll be back as soon as I can. A team of Belgian horses couldn't keep me away. Besides, I have to make up for my pathetic attempt at love making tonight."

"I think it was great. I'm happy you were so excited. I hope that excitement never wears off," Emily whispered in his ear before she said goodnight.

Luke stood quietly after the door closed. He had the urge to go after her, to gather her in his arms and never let her go. Reluctantly, he turned and slowly made his way down the steps and out to his car.

On the ride back to the farm, Luke relived the events of the evening. He berated himself for being so immature and climaxing before he barely got started. It wasn't that he was unfamiliar with orgasms. He'd had a number of them. It wasn't difficult to become excited thinking about the raven haired beauty he once had a childhood crush on.

Burdine Poole was a lot older and a great deal taller. She was also four grades ahead of him. They used to walk home together from the one room schoolhouse that sat on a corner of the Canfield farm. It wasn't that she walked with *him*, exactly. She was just one of eight kids who lived farther down the road.

Since his house was closest to the school. Luke was the first to peel off from the group. He often wished he lived farther away so he could spend more time with her. He always tried to make the most of their short walk by sticking as close to her as he dared, but she never seemed to notice. That didn't stop him from dreaming about her at night, or thinking about her every waking minute of every day.

He recalled the day he got too close and accidentally bumped into her. She caught him before he fell.

She smiled broadly. It was a beautiful smile. And it was aimed directly at him.

"Are you okay, Luke?" she asked.

He moved away and hurried into his driveway without saying a word.

He had trouble falling asleep that night. He kept beating himself up. Finally, an opportunity to strike up a conversation with the girl of his dreams and he was too shy to say a word.

There never seemed to be another opportunity to speak with her. She graduated from eighth grade and he never saw her again.

Luke's feelings for her had faded over the years, but he still thought about her from time to time. He wondered where she was and if she had married. He hoped she was as happy as he was feeling right now.

He put the thoughts of Burdine aside. No longer would he have to fantasize about making love with a girl. This was the real thing. For an instant, he panicked. This was his first orgasm as a result of sexual intercourse. What if it happened again? What if he was unable to wait until Emily was satisfied? No woman would put up with that. If he wasn't able to control his excitement, his next date with her may be his last.

I wonder what she would have done if I'd been wearing bib overalls instead of dress pants? He chuckled at the thought. *It probably would have been safer for both of us.*

***

Monday morning, less than three months after their interlude with the chicken ring and their first attempt at making love, Emily was sick. She'd been vomiting all morning. Her mother stayed home from work to take her to the doctor to get the test results from a week earlier when she'd displayed the same symptoms.

"Is it the flu, Doctor?" Eleanor asked as Dr. Freedman finished his examination.

The doctor smiled. "No, it's something far more serious. But she should be just fine in a few more months. Young lady, you are about two months pregnant," he calmly announced.

Emily beamed. She was ecstatic. She could hardly control herself. She wanted to dance and shout and tell the whole world. She wasn't really surprised by the announcement. After the failed attempt the night Luke proposed, they had made love nearly every time they got together. It usually occurred in the front seat of his car, but sometimes in her bedroom. He never used condoms and he never withdrew before he climaxed. Best of all, he always let her finish first. She glanced at her mother.

Eleanor's mouth fell open. She didn't seem at all happy. She was pale at first, obviously shocked by the news. But color crept slowly back into her face. It turned red. Emily had seen that look before. Her mother was fuming.

Even though the ride home was a ten-minute drive, it seemed to Emily it would never end. Her mother started the lecture as soon as they were in the car.

"I can't believe you would be so irresponsible," Eleanor said through clenched teeth. "You're only seventeen. You had your whole life ahead of you and you threw it all away on some farm boy. Haven't you learned anything about men?" She stepped on the gas and sped out of the parking lot as if racing to distance herself from the origin of bad news.

Eleanor wheeled her Chevy coupe down Randolph, across Highway 218, and up the hill to South Street, all the while smoldering over the obvious mistake her daughter had made. "Why not Max Gordon? He was an intelligent young man with a bright future...and he was crazy about you."

"I wasn't in love with Max Gordon. I won't marry anyone

I'm not in love with. I don't care who they are." Emily pounded the seat with her fist. Her breath caught in her throat. If her mother only knew what kind of an animal Max Gordon was, she wouldn't keep bringing up his name. Or maybe she would just blame her daughter. Emily was in a no-win situation.

"But a farmer? You have nothing in common with a farmer." Eleanor slammed on the brakes to avoid a car backing out of a private drive.

Emily was glad her mother was watching the road. She never felt comfortable looking the fiery woman in the eyes when she was angry.

The last few blocks were covered in silence, and by the time they pulled up to the house, Eleanor appeared resigned to the inevitable.

"Well, you have no choice now," she sighed. "You'll have to marry him. And since you're already two months pregnant, the sooner the better."

***

Emily was sitting on the steps of the front porch when Luke pulled up. They often sat on the porch when he came to visit. It was quiet and more private than inside with her mother and a renter who occupied part of the second floor.

It was a lover's evening with a gentle summer breeze. The sun had set, but the street lights hadn't come on yet. Large oak trees on the sloped lawn provided the perfect romantic setting to announce the new life she was carrying.

Emily smiled as Luke approached. He had obviously been working in the sun. He had a darker tan than a week ago.

She fought an impulse to jump up, run to him and shout she was pregnant with his child. The first of many, she hoped. She was aglow. Maybe he would notice.

He strolled up the walk, took a seat beside her and gave her a kiss. As Emily responded in kind, she wondered if Luke could tell this particular kiss was more complete. Her whole body and soul had participated. They didn't speak. They just clung to each other.

"I'm pregnant," she whispered.

He didn't respond. He must not have heard. "Did you hear me? I'm pregnant." Emily pulled away and gazed into his eyes.

"That's...great," he stammered.

He didn't look like he thought it was good news. Color drained from his face. He turned his head and sat quietly.

Emily clung to his arm. She had expected a more enthusiastic response. What was he thinking? *Surely, he's happy about the pregnancy, too.*

Luke slowly rose to his feet and took Emily by the hands, gazing into her eyes.

"I fell in love with you, and I made up my mind I was going to marry you, the minute I saw you in the theater," he said with a sheepish grin. "I also intended for us to have a bunch of kids. I just hadn't figured on it being this soon."

He pulled her to her feet and held her close.

"I love you," he said as their lips met.

After a few more kisses and a long embrace, Luke said enthusiastically, "We'd better go celebrate. I'll buy you an ice cream cone."

"Last of the big spenders." She chuckled. "You must have read my mind. That's exactly what I want. But I have to go to the bathroom first." She grabbed Luke's hand and walked with him into the house.

Eleanor met them in the living room. She didn't say anything, not even hello. She glared at her daughter's boyfriend as though he was a thief who had come to rob her. Emily clung to his arm as Luke stood silently by.

"When are you two getting married?" The words spat from Eleanor's mouth as though she'd tasted some bad food.

"Well...I...don't know," Luke stammered.

He didn't feel comfortable in Eleanor's presence. She had never come right out and said so, but on the few occasions they had spoken, he got the feeling she didn't like him.

"How about two weeks from tomorrow?" Eleanor's words were more than a question. They were a mandate.

"Well...that sounds good to me," he managed to say.

"I'll make the arrangements," Eleanor said. She quickly turned and left the room.

Luke was still standing speechless when Emily released his arm and hurried to the bathroom. She knew he hadn't planned on marriage so soon. She would be eighteen in a few more days, but he wouldn't be twenty-one for another four months. He needed his parents' permission to get married. Emily smiled at the thought; thankful the confrontation with her mother had ended, at least for the time being.

***

It was a simple ceremony, held at the Episcopal Church where Emily and her mother had been attending. Emily wore her best dress and Luke wore the same dress pants and tie that he'd worn for his high school graduation picture. Luke's brother, Henry, and Emily's friend, Laura, served as best man and bridesmaid. Mothers of the bride and groom were the only other people in attendance.

Afterwards, Luke dropped Emily off at her mother's house before hurrying back to the farm. The cows needed milking and the hogs needed to be fed.

After the chores were done, Luke climbed into his car and headed for town. His mind churned through the day's events. This morning, he was responsible only to himself. But now, he was married with a baby on the way. How in the hell was he going to support a wife and baby on fifty dollars a month? He would have to ask his father for more money. Maybe even get another job.

Emily's allergies to hay and corn pollen prevented her from living at the farm, so Emily's mother had agreed to let them live with her. Luke doubted that would last long, seeing as how she frequently acted as if she could barely tolerate his presence. He had conflicting thoughts about his situation. He resented the fact that he was forced to get married before he was ready, but it was his own fault. He should have acted more responsibly. He should have taken precautions. He should have paid attention to detail.

It seemed strange that he would be sleeping somewhere other than the old farmhouse where he'd spent every night since the day he was born. He would just have to get used to it. He shook his head. He would have to get used to a lot of things.

***

Rebecca was born in March. It was a happy time at first, but now there was another mouth to feed and diapers to wash. Emily's mother and Luke were at work, and Emily was left to care for the baby. But Rebecca cried a lot, especially at night. Emily couldn't stay up all day and half the night too, so Luke would often spend several hours each night rocking or holding the baby. Eleanor also took her turn. Lack of sleep kept everyone on edge.

It had been another trying day. Emily had just warmed the baby bottle and settled onto the couch with Rebecca in her arms when Luke came in and eased down beside her.

"How did your day go?" she asked.

"I joined the Army," he calmly said.

Emily pulled the nipple from the baby's mouth, placed the bottle on the coffee table, and glared at her husband.

"You...what?"

"I joined the Army."

Emily looked away and sat quietly until Rebecca started to fuss. She picked up the bottle and guided the nipple into the baby's mouth.

"When are you leaving?"

"The 23rd of August. A week after our first wedding anniversary," he softly replied.

"Why the Army?" she asked.

"Well, we can't live with your mother forever," Luke said. "I can't see any other way out. My dad wants me at the farm more and you complain that I'm gone too much. It's like my legs are tied to teams of horses pulling in opposite directions. I have to do something or be torn completely apart. Besides, your mother will probably be glad I'm gone. It'll be one less mouth to feed."

"What's your father going to say?" Emily asked. "Who's going to help him on the farm?"

"I don't know. He'll just have to hire someone," Luke replied.

Emily's eyes started to well up. "I don't know how I'm going to get along without you," she sniffled.

Luke put his arm around her. "I'm sure you'll be just fine. Maybe I can figure out a way so you and Becky can join me once I get settled. They were telling me at the recruiting station that military housing was available for families."

Each sat quietly until the baby bottle was empty and Rebecca was asleep. Luke took her from Emily's arms and placed her gently in her crib. Emily hoped she would stay asleep, at least for a few hours. She and Luke still had lots to talk about.

***

The following morning, Luke left for the farm earlier than usual. His explanation of why he joined the Army went over with Emily much better than he'd expected. He hoped it would go as well with his father. It was a drastic decision he was making. Never in his wildest dreams had he ever considered joining the military. He had planned to remain a farmer forever.

As soon as he turned off the highway and onto the gravel road that led to the farm, the car's tires began kicking up pebbles that pinged off the undercarriage of the car, creating a hypnotic cadence.

He glanced in his rearview mirror at the swirling mass that trailed behind. He suddenly felt as insignificant and helpless as the cloud of dust swept up by the force of his moving car. His life was turning out just as chaotic and uncontrollable. His senses told him big changes were in store. Forces beyond his control were guiding him in the direction of his destiny. And like the particles of dust and sand kicked up by his moving car, only fate would determine where he would finally land.

PART THREE – THE ROOKIE

"There is no such thing as chance; and what seems to us merest
accident springs from the deepest source of destiny."
– Freidrich Shiller. German dramatist, poet and historian
(1759-1805)

CHAPTER THREE

Phoenix, Arizona

Spring 1963

Phoenix Police Officer, Luke Canfield, guided the Studebaker Lark through the dimly lit parking lot of the Sunnyslope briefing station. He slowed before exiting onto Dunlap Avenue to avoid a group of boisterous pedestrians making their way into Brookshire's.

It was handy for officers to share a parking lot with a restaurant. But since it was the only one in the area open all night, it was a magnet for drunks trying to sober up on coffee before their drive home from the local bars. This resulted in frequent calls of "drunk disturbing," especially on Friday and Saturday nights. All incoming calls, however, were routed to the downtown station and dispatched from there, so the disturbance was often quelled by the time an officer arrived. The briefing station was merely a location where officers gathered at shift change to receive their assignments and pick up their equipment. The last one out locked the door.

Luke didn't like working nights, but patrol officers changed shifts every two months. Besides, he was still a probationer, and would be for the next seven months, so he'd better not complain about anything.

Everyone was on probation for the first year of employment. That meant he could be fired at any time, even for the smallest infraction, and there wasn't a damned thing he could do about it. But Luke wasn't concerned about that. He felt comfortable in his training and his ability.

He'd spent the first four months on the job in West Phoenix. But a month ago, he was transferred to Sunnyslope in order to become familiar with the northern part of the city. At least that's what the transfer order said. But Luke knew better. He lived a stone's throw from the Maryvale briefing station and it was no secret that the brass didn't like an officer living in the area he was assigned to patrol.

It seemed strange not to have a senior partner telling him

what to do and how to do it. He'd had one since his transfer.

Luke had confidence in Fred Sloan. Fred seemed to know everything about everything and was always one step ahead of a developing problem. But his partner had taken the night off. And since the squad was short-handed, Luke was riding solo.

Sergeant Bill Richards was a brusque, old-school supervisor who didn't mince words. He was built like a bull with arms like fence posts. Even at middle age, he looked like he could easily handle himself in a physical confrontation.

"Canfield," the sergeant barked, "your baby-sitter is off tonight. Do you think you can find your way to your beat and back all by yourself without getting lost?"

"I think so," Luke hesitantly replied.

"You don't sound very sure of yourself," Richards growled.

"I'm sure, Sarge. No problem."

The car keys Richards tossed in Luke's direction skidded across the table and onto the floor as the hapless probationer made a feeble attempt to grab them.

"I hope you're better at catching crooks than you are at catching car keys. Keep your head out of your ass and your eyes on the road. And stay out of trouble. Creech, you watch out for him."

Officer Dennis Creech was the classic example of a

ladies man with his lean frame, fine features, and long black hair combed straight back. When Luke first met him, his initial thought was that Creech looked out of place in a police uniform. In fact, there was something about him that seemed out of place with the entire human race. Luke couldn't put his finger on it, but Dennis Creech was different than anyone he'd ever met. And far more irritating.

Creech rolled his eyes and shot his sergeant a disapproving glance before turning his attention back to the Blue Book, a large hardcover binder where teletype messages were kept.

The first one in the station at the beginning of shift was required to tear the most recent pages from the teletype machine near the lieutenant's office and place them in the Blue Book. Either the squad sergeant or one of the officers would read the latest messages on stolen cars, burglaries, and other crime related information to the squad as part of their briefing.

What bothered Luke about the whole thing was that the cover of the book wasn't even blue. It was green. He mentioned his observation one day.

"Why is it called the *Blue* Book when it's green? I would think it would be called the *Green* Book."

Creech again rolled his eyes and glared at the newbie. "Who the hell cares what color the damn book is? What matters is what's inside."

"The cover changes from time to time, depending on how long it lasts, but the teletype print is always blue. That's why we call it the Blue Book," Fred Sloan quietly explained.

That was an important lesson for Luke. He would be more careful, not only about the questions he asked, but whom he asked. Still, it was a funny thing. He sensed that Creech was by far the most intelligent person there, but for some reason he deliberately concealed it with obnoxious comments.

Even though Creech seemed to go out of his way to alienate the rookie, Luke felt a connection in some way. It was like they had been brothers in another life. Yet, whenever Luke tried to use his powers of insight with Creech, he drew a blank. He had no idea what was going on in the man's head. He quickly dismissed the thought of having close ties with Dennis Creech. It was too ridiculous to even consider. *Why in the hell would I feel connected to that weirdo? The only thing we have in common is the uniform.*

It was a quiet night even for a Thursday. Traffic was light as Luke crept slowly along Dunlap Avenue to 7th Street.

He hung a right and a few blocks south he came to the 24-hour donut shop. His beat was actually farther north, but it was mostly desert out there and no place to eat during the night shift. No one got too upset if the northernmost units drifted south.

He would love to have stopped for a cup of coffee, but it was too early for a break and he couldn't take a chance on missing a radio call. As he drove slowly past the donut shop, two young men standing by their cars laughed as they held their hands to their ears and wiggled their fingers.

Luke was forced to smile. Everyone poked fun at the cartoon-looking police cars with their round, flat, red lights that resembled the ears on Mickey Mouse. People who were pulled over by the funny-looking little cars, however, didn't find them amusing.

It was after midnight and Luke didn't have much on his worksheet. He'd checked the doors and windows of a few businesses to make sure they hadn't been burglarized. He had also staked out an intersection for red light runners. But everyone seemed to be obeying the law. It was as if the public was deliberately making his life difficult. He needed a line for his worksheet or his sergeant would be on him. Everyone was expected to make an entry of police activity at least once an hour.

The whole city seemed to be asleep. There hadn't been any radio transmissions for quite some time. If only he would get a call. Any call. He'd even be happy with a barking dog call. At least he would have a legitimate entry for his worksheet. Maybe the radio wasn't working. He turned the squelch button. Loud static proved it was. He settled back and continued down the deserted street.

"The time is 1:00 a.m. KOA789."

The dispatcher's calm voice broke the stillness. It was a welcome sound. Luke wished she would repeat it just so he could hear her voice again. The dispatcher was his protector. She may have been miles away in a physical sense, but emotionally, she was riding right along beside him. Notification of the time, however, didn't put a line on his worksheet. It was going to be a long night.

The quiet streets gave Luke too much time to relive the nightmare of his youth and the chain of events that led him to his present position as an officer with the Phoenix police department.

No matter how hard he tried to concentrate on the brighter side of things, darker thoughts always muscled their way in.

How could something that happened when he was nine years old seem like it was only yesterday? There was some consolation in the fact that he'd saved his little sister from drowning. But he had never been able to explain the voice in his head that warned him Evy was in danger when he was in the barn and she was out of sight across the yard. It was too strange to even think about, let alone try to explain. But from that moment on, Luke knew he was different.

The trauma had triggered an ability he refused to accept, even though it kept cropping up like weeds in a cornfield: the ability to feel the turmoil and sense the fear in the minds of others.

Luke was a died-in-the-wool pragmatist. Everything happened for a reason. Everything had a rational explanation. Everything that is, except for this. His mind was in turmoil whenever he tried to rationalize the phenomenon so he tried not to think about it.

There were other thoughts, however, that plagued his mind. Thoughts that were equally difficult to process.

Joining the army had been a welcome relief from the tug of war between his wife and his father. But returning to Waterloo after his enlistment was up put him right back in the same situation. He tried to break the psychological hold with the farm by driving truck for an oil company. But he couldn't deny his relief when his father's hired hand quit and Luke was asked to help out with the crops. He was finally back where he belonged. His roots to the land were as deeply embedded as the giant cottonwood that shaded the schoolhouse on the corner of the farm. Family illness, however, forced him to rethink his priorities.

He needed to move to a drier climate, the doctor said. The bouts of asthma and hay fever that his wife and son experienced were becoming more frequent and more severe. What else could he do but load up the family and move to Arizona? Any responsible husband and father would have done the same.

The death of his sister, Evelyn, was the final straw. Although the doctor hadn't said her early death was the result of near drowning when she was three years old, Luke was sure it was. He was equally sure it was his fault. He would move away and start a new life. There was nothing left to hold him to the land he swore he'd never leave. Painful memories were all that remained.

He had never considered becoming a police officer until he got to Phoenix and found nothing else available. There was no other choice. He had a family to support.

His thoughts jumped back and forth between the memories of his past and his need to log something on his worksheet. But how could he put something down if there was nothing going on?

He would have to be creative without making a false entry. He'd heard of officers driving through a cemetery and taking names from headstones to put on their worksheet as a citizen contact. But there weren't any cemeteries on his beat, and that wasn't something he would do anyway. Maybe something would crop up after he had a cup of coffee.

The donut shop was empty when Luke strolled in. That

suited him just fine. He preferred the quiet atmosphere of the little donut shop to the noisy hustle and bustle of Brookshire's. He could drink his coffee in peace without having to contend with some obnoxious drunk.

After a few minutes, the baker came out of the back room.

"How's it going tonight?" Luke asked.

"Slow, but that's OK. I gotta lotta work ta do. My helper didn't show. What can I get ya?"

Joe Cleets was a big man; taller than Luke's 6' 2," and some forty pounds heavier. Luke had met him before when he and Sloan had stopped in for coffee. He had a once-white apron draped around his jellyroll belly that was smeared with a variety of colors.

Luke grinned. It wouldn't take much of a detective to determine the most recent flavors he'd been working with.

"A cup of coffee with cream–lots of cream–and whatever your freshest donut is," Luke replied. He climbed onto one of the stools at the counter and again examined the baker's apron for the most likely flavors.

"Got some raspberry-filled that I just pulled from the fryer," Joe announced as he headed for the kitchen.

"Sounds great. My favorite," Luke replied.

After serving the coffee and donut, Joe motioned to the

coffee pot and the display case of day-old pastries. "Help yourself to more coffee and anything in the case. I'd better get back to my baking."

"What do I owe you?" Luke asked.

"Nothin'. On the house. Glad you guys stop by at night." Joe hurried off to the back room.

Luke drained his cup and poured another as he eyed his watch to make sure he didn't go over his ten minute break. After finishing his coffee, he fished in his pocket and pulled out some change. Two quarters, three dimes and a nickel.

He always carried some dimes in case he had to use a pay phone. If an officer went through the city's main switchboard, the coin was returned, so most had a dime tucked away somewhere. But Luke made sure he had at least two in case his coin wasn't returned. It wouldn't do for a probationer to get caught short.

Most restaurants offered free coffee to cops, especially the ones open all night. The uniform headed off a lot of trouble. Most cops accepted. But Luke never liked the idea. It was his belief that nothing was free. There was always a catch. So he made it a point to leave enough money to cover the cost as well as the tip. He placed thirty cents beside his empty cup.

After checking a few more businesses to make sure he hadn't missed any burglaries, Luke slowly made his way down 7th

Street.

He was already tired and it was only 2 a.m. He wouldn't get off for another four hours. He'd looked for a car to stop. But none he'd seen so far had given him any reason, and he couldn't just stop a car because he needed a line on his worksheet.

As he approached the Arizona canal, one of nine waterways that cut their way across the valley floor, a cloud of dust boiled up from a car that had peeled off the gravel road along the canal bank and headed south on 7th Street. That road was restricted to maintenance vehicles. "No Trespassing" signs were posted at each intersection.

"Finally, a reason to stop a car," Luke murmured. He hurriedly caught up to the '59 Chevy and flipped on his overheads.

After a short distance, the Chevy pulled to the side of the road and stopped. Luke shone his spotlight on the back window, but the sunscreen that many drivers in Arizona had installed to block the penetrating sun prevented him from seeing inside.

Luke had a strange feeling. A voice in his head told him to be careful. It was eerily similar to the voice that had warned him about his little sister's near drowning so many years before. He picked up the mic.

"Six-ten." His voice sounded strange.

"Six-ten," Sandstorm Sandy acknowledged.

The nickname officers had bestowed on the dispatcher was well grounded. Her voice wasn't the most pleasant, but she was one of the most competent, and officers felt safe with her.

"Six-ten, I'll be Code-6 with a blue '59 Chevy, 7th Street and the Arizona Canal. An Arizona plate, but it's in the back window and covered with sunscreen."

"10-4. Do you want another unit?"

Luke was urged to say, hell yes. Send one immediately.

"Not at this time," he said.

"10-4," the dispatcher replied.

Luke scribbled a description of the Chevy on his notepad and slowly stepped out of his vehicle. His apprehension, he told himself, was because this was his first stop. He would give the driver a warning and at least have a legitimate entry for his worksheet. It was probably just a couple of lovers. They often used the darkened canal bank for intimate activity. Nothing to be alarmed about.

As he reached the halfway point between his car and the Chevy, an invisible force stopped him in his tracks. He stumbled back, unsure of what had just happened. He must have imagined it. His mind played tricks on him from time to time. But that cautionary voice in his head wouldn't go away.

He retreated to his patrol car and sat with one foot on the ground. He grabbed the mic, but quickly slammed it back in its cradle. He would be ribbed mercilessly if he asked for a backup just to check out a couple of lovers. No, he would have to do this alone. He must have just imagined he'd run into an invisible wall. He would ignore the feeling and do his job.

Luke strode briskly towards the Chevy, but was stopped again at the same spot by an invisible force. The voice in his head told him to retreat to the safety of his car. He backed slowly toward his patrol car, his right hand on his gun, his eyes glued to the driver's side of the Chevy.

As he opened his car door, Luke glimpsed an arm extend from the driver's side of the open back window of the Chevy and a muzzle flash as a bullet whizzed by his head.

"What the hell!" Luke yelped as he dove into his car to escape the hail of bullets.

Tires squealed and gravel flew as the Chevy tore off down the road.

Without conscious thought, Luke slammed the Lark into drive, activated the siren, and chased after the fleeing vehicle, steering with one hand while calmly keying the mic with the other.

"Six-ten, I'm in pursuit of a blue '59 Chevy, south on 7th

Street from the Arizona canal. They just shot at me."

An ear piercing wail blasted from the radio; an alert to warn all cars an emergency transmission would immediately follow.

"All units," the dispatcher responded just as calmly. "Six-ten is in pursuit of a blue 1959 Chevy, south on 7th Street from the Arizona canal. Shots fired."

"They just turned right on Northern," Luke said.

"West on Northern Avenue from 7th Street," the dispatcher relayed.

Something was hitting the front of his car. Luke thought it was pebbles being kicked up by the fleeing vehicle, but he soon realized it was something far more deadly.

"They're still shooting at me." His voice was calm and unhurried. Even though he was being shot at, he felt in control.

"Tell Six-ten to keep us informed of the major intersections he passes," Sergeant Richards bellowed. "Where are they now?"

"Six-ten, what's your location now?" the dispatcher calmly asked.

Luke would like to have told her, but he didn't have a clue, other than they were still going west on Northern.

"Past 7th Avenue. Still westbound," the officer Luke had seen at the last intersection calmly advised. It was the voice of

Dennis Creech.

Luke silently thanked him. It took some immediate heat off. But he'd better pay attention to where he was or there'd be hell to pay.

"Past 7th Avenue, westbound," the dispatcher repeated.

"If anyone spots the chase, let us know where and what direction so Six-ten can keep his hands on the wheel," Sergeant Richards barked.

Luke was relieved that his sergeant was looking out for his welfare. Maybe he wasn't such a hard-ass after all.

"Past 19th Avenue, still westbound." Shots echoed through the mic when an officer yelled the location.

"Be careful with your shots so you don't hit Six-ten," Richards growled.

That was the first time Luke had heard stress in his sergeant's voice.

"Westbound over the freeway. Still shooting at me," Luke announced. He easily recognized that location. It wasn't difficult as I-17 was the only north and south freeway through town. The dispatcher relayed his directions.

Luke saw brake lights as the Chevy spun around the corner. "South on 27th Avenue," he coolly announced as he glimpsed the street sign.

"South on 27ᵗʰ Avenue from Northern," dispatch relayed.

"Tell Six-ten not to get too close. Just keep them in sight. If they continue south we'll box them in at the railroad tracks," Sergeant Richards directed.

"Copied." Luke responded before the message could be relayed.

"They just flew past Glendale," an officer reported, followed by the same transmission from the dispatcher.

"Past Bethany. Still southbound," an officer at that location shouted.

"Past Bethany Home Road, still southbound," the dispatcher mimicked.

"Past Camelback." Luke's transmission was relayed to the other units as he continued the chase.

He had checked his speedometer from time to time, and with the gas pedal clear to the floor, all he could coax out of the Lark was eighty-five miles per hour. Apparently, the Chevy couldn't do any better. He was able to keep on its tail.

"Past Indian School Road, still southbound." Luke easily recognized that location. It used to be his beat area when he worked out of the Maryvale briefing station, a small modified house that sat on the north side of the road just west of the intersection.

A short while later, an array of flashing red lights and a cloud of dust ahead caused Luke to slam on his brakes and slide to a halt. He quickly killed the siren and leaped from his vehicle.

The Chevy had left the road and crashed through a fence just north of where 27th Avenue, Thomas Road, and Grand Avenue came together.

Other officers were already at the car pulling out the driver as Luke ran up.

"Where's the other one? The one who was in the back seat doing all the shooting?" Luke asked after glancing inside the vehicle.

"We didn't see anyone else," Creech mocked. "Maybe you just imagined it. First night riding by yourself and all."

There was no mistaking the voice of Dennis Creech, who had advised radio of the pursuit passing 7th Avenue and Northern, so how the hell did he get to the scene of the crash so fast. There was no way he could have gotten there ahead of the lead car. Yet, here he was. Luke shook it off. He had no time to think of Dennis Creech. The shooter was still on the loose.

"Search the area," Sergeant Richards yelled after examining the bullet holes in Luke's patrol car. "He's got to be close by."

The officers fanned out and began the search.

Luke moved slowly and methodically, his Colt .38 in one

hand and his flashlight in the other, probing every inch of the rocky, tumbleweed, and sagebrush strewn area.

As he approached a large creosote bush, a voice in his head cautioned him to stop. He immediately pulled up and remained motionless, listening for any sound. He held his flashlight away from his body and shone it into the bush.

Luke knew the suspect was near. He sensed danger. It radiated from the bush like heat from a furnace. Every fiber in Luke's body was poised for action as he visually explored the vegetation.

"Drop that gun and come outta there," an officer on the opposite side of the bush yelled.

Luke's first thought was that the officer had mistaken him for the suspect. Before he could respond, the man they'd been searching for crawled out from under the bush and laid his gun on the ground. Dennis Creech had him at gunpoint.

Well. Do you still think it's my imagination, you dumb ass? That's what Luke wanted to say. But Creech probably did save his life, so maybe he'd better be a little more thankful.

He whipped out his cuffs, but Creech shook his head and extended his own. "My arrest. My cuffs."

Once an ass. Always an ass. Luke couldn't help the thought as he put his own cuffs away and slapped the ones on that Creech had offered.

After the suspect was placed securely in Creech's patrol car, Luke returned to his own vehicle.

He counted five bullet holes. Three in the left fender and two near the top of the radiator.

"Damn! That was close," he muttered. "What the hell were they shooting at me for? I was just going to give them a warning for trespassing. Now they're going to jail for attempted murder. Idiots."

He slid behind the wheel and sat quietly, his thoughts on the invisible wall that had kept him from walking up to the suspect's vehicle and being shot. There must be a rational explanation. Maybe he'd imagined the whole thing. His training must have kicked in without his conscious effort. But what about the man Creech caught? Luke had stopped just in time with that one too. One more step might have been his last. And how the hell did Creech get to the scene before Luke, when Luke was the lead car and Creech had been sitting at 7th Avenue and Northern when the chase went by. He shook his head and started the engine, refusing to waste any more time trying to figure something out that was impossible to explain.

He swung the Lark slowly around and headed for the station. Sergeant Richards had assigned another unit to stand by for the wrecker that would haul the Chevy to the evidence impound lot. But Luke had a lengthy report to write and the Identification Bureau to call. Pictures had to be taken of the bullet holes in his car, and sometimes the I-Bureau was slow to respond.

Luke pulled into the station parking lot and sat quietly for a few minutes, his mind awash with thoughts of how close he came to losing his life. It was strange that he wasn't afraid, even after being shot at. Maybe he'd used up all of his fear while in the paratroops.

He was scared to death of heights, but he never regretted his decision to transfer from regular Army to Airborne. The hazardous duty pay supplemented his regular income and provided enough money for an apartment so Emily and Rebecca could live with him off base. He reminded himself of that fact before each terror-stricken jump. That was the only thing that got him out the door. It would have been ironic, however, to have been killed while doing something that didn't scare him as opposed to something that terrified him. He dismissed the thought as he gathered up his equipment and strolled into the station.

***

Emily Canfield put the kids to bed and settled down with *The New Yorker*. It was her favorite time of day; one of the few times she did what she wanted instead of what was required as a mother of three kids and the wife of a cop. She enjoyed the intellectual cartoons and enlightening articles that the magazine provided.

Emily seldom thought about her childhood, at least not on a conscious level. But those dark days simmered just below the surface, ready to boil over if given half a chance.

How could something that happened when she was eleven still bother her? Maybe she deserved to be haunted. Her father would still be alive today if she hadn't wished and prayed so hard he would die.

She should have forgiven him for the physical abuse to her mother and herself. After all, he had always apologized after one of his drunken tirades. When he asked forgiveness before he crashed his car, she should have given him one more chance to make good on his promise to quit drinking.

Terrifying memories of the past often crept into her consciousness when she least expected it. She tried to keep them at bay by thinking pleasant thoughts. The one she relied on the most was the day she and Luke first met.

It always brought a smile to her face whenever she thought

about that shy, bib overall-clad farm boy who had quietly eased down beside her in the movie theater on that rainy spring day.

It had been a long and sometimes difficult journey while married to Luke. She loved him dearly, but he seemed absorbed with his work; obsessed with the smallest detail. She wished he would pay that much attention to his family.

All probationers were restricted from working a second job, so their budget was stretched thin. In addition, Luke came up with the down payment on a trailer house for her mother when she moved to Phoenix, even though the two had never really hit it off.

Emily was grateful he had offered the money and never complained about making the monthly payments. Luke joked he was glad to do it rather than have his mother-in-law live with them. But Emily suspected there was a good deal of truth in what he'd said. The added financial burden, however, required careful spending. Four hundred and twenty dollars a month didn't go very far for a family of five.

Emily knew her husband was working all of the overtime he could get so she could stay home and raise the kids. Two girls and a boy required a lot of time and effort.

Still, she didn't like to have him away so much, especially at night. It was too lonely in bed without him. Not only that, but she worried about his safety. Darkness seemed to bring out the worst in people, and if there was danger, Luke was liable to walk right into it.

He was the bravest and strongest man she'd ever known. She knew he was deathly afraid of heights, yet he had joined the paratroops because it paid more than the regular army. The extra money made it possible for Rebecca and her to join him. She would never forget his sacrifice.

Emily never doubted Luke's love or his commitment to his family. She just wished he would keep a low profile at work and stay home more.

With a heavy sigh through pursed lips, she put aside her magazine and made ready for bed. She probably worried for nothing. Luke was likely sitting in some restaurant making nice with the waitress.

She quickly put the thought out of her head. Thinking like that would keep her awake all night. She slipped into bed and curled up on Luke's side. It made her feel closer to him and relaxed her mind as she drifted off to sleep.

***

After getting Rebecca and Michael off to school, and Amy

back to sleep after a restless night, Emily poured herself a cup of coffee and glanced at the clock. Eight-thirty. Luke's shift ended at six. He should have been home long ago. What if something had happened? Surely the department would have notified her immediately. Bad news always travels fast. Maybe he just got bogged down with paperwork. He often used that excuse when he was late. No, if it was just paperwork he would have called.

Maybe she should call the station. She picked up the phone, but placed it back in its cradle without dialing. Luke didn't like her to call unless it was an emergency. Some wives called too often and their husbands were the butt of jokes. Besides, Luke was still on probation and the department might think his wife was meddling and fire him. She would just have to wait.

He'd better have a damned good excuse for being late and not calling. He knew how worried she would get. She tried to calm herself by gazing through the kitchen window. The passion vines along the west wall of the carport usually soothed her. Their gorgeous purple flowers made her feel all was right with the world. This morning, however, they had little effect.

***

It was nearing 9:30 a.m. when Luke pulled into his

driveway. Until that moment, he hadn't realized how completely exhausted he was.

He stepped slowly out of his vehicle and headed for the door, unsure how to explain the night's events to Emily. She worried enough as it was. She would really flip out if he told her how close he came to getting his head blown off. He dismissed the idea of not telling her. She would eventually hear about it anyway and wonder what else he hadn't told her. He was still trying to come up with a softer version as he reached the door.

Luke braced himself and slowly opened the door, still undecided exactly how to tell Emily he'd been involved in a running gun battle.

As he stepped inside, she ran to greet him and threw her arms around his neck, trembling as she held him tight.

"Hey. What's going on? Are you all right?" he asked.

She released her grip and stepped back, her eyes watery and her lips quivering. "I was going to ask you the same thing," she quickly replied. "What happened to you? I had the strangest feeling that you were in trouble. Then when you didn't come home, I was sure of it. But I was too scared to call the station. I didn't want to hear the bad news. Why didn't you call and tell me you were going to be late? Are you trying to drive me completely crazy?"

Luke stepped closer, but Emily pulled back and hurried to the kitchen.

"I'm sorry," he said while following closely behind. "I thought I could get things wrapped up sooner. I had a lot of paperwork and I had to wait for I-Bureau to come out and take some pictures. I should have called. I'm sorry."

Emily poured him a cup of coffee and set it on the table.

"Did you eat?" she asked.

"No. I could use a couple eggs and some toast."

He got the milk from the refrigerator and splashed some in his coffee before settling down at the table.

As Emily prepared breakfast, Luke explained the night's events, careful not to get too dramatic about it.

"I stopped a car coming off the canal bank. The occupants fired some shots into the fender of my police car. I guess they were aiming for the radiator so that I couldn't follow them."

"Somebody shot at you?" Emily gasped as she turned to face her husband. "Are you hurt?"

"No, I'm not hurt. They were just shooting at my car," Luke hurriedly replied. "We caught them both, but I still don't know why they were so desperate to get away. They were probably up to no good or were wanted for something. I'll probably find out tonight what they were up to."

"I hate that job," Emily groused. "I don't know why you couldn't have been a bank…er…well…not that exactly, but something where you wouldn't have to risk your life every day."

"You mean like Max?" Luke couldn't help the retort. Emily's mother had mentioned early on that Maxwell Gordon, a banker's son, was the husband of choice for her daughter. Eleanor had been adamantly opposed to Emily marrying a no-account farm boy.

"I mean like a normal person. Someone who works normal business hours and comes home every night." Emily slid the plate of eggs and toast across the table.

"You do have a point," Luke said.

He sprinkled some salt and a copious amount of pepper on his fried eggs. "Sometimes I think I picked the wrong line of work. But…it puts eggs and toast on the table…and coffee. I could use another cup." He grinned as he mopped up some yolk with a piece of toast and stuffed it into his mouth.

He stifled the urge to tell Emily that he didn't have a choice as to what kind of job he took. He was only nine years old when his destiny was determined. The job picked him.

CHAPTER FOUR

The following night, most of the squad was already busy with paperwork when Luke strolled quietly in.

"Well, the man-of-the-hour decided to grace us with his presence again tonight," Creech exclaimed. "We were taking bets you wouldn't show after nearly getting your head blown off last night."

Luke took a seat at the briefing table. He tried to ignore the comment, but Creech's presence always made his blood boil, even when he was silent.

"All in a night's work," Luke replied.

"Boy, I take one night off and miss all the action," Sloan groused. "That was a first rate job you did last night. Wish I had been there."

"I have a good training officer," Luke quickly replied. "I just asked myself what Fred Sloan would do and everything turned out all right. Except I managed to get your car shot full of holes."

"Hazards of the job," Sloan replied. "Bullet holes in cars can be easily repaired. The ones in people not so much."

Other members of the squad complimented Luke on his calmness under fire. They were joined by Sergeant Richards.

"It was probably a good thing you didn't know who you were chasing last night," the sergeant growled, "or we might have heard a little more urgency in your transmissions. You showed no more emotion than if you were reporting a dead cat in the street."

Sergeant Richards glanced at a paper he was holding. "They were some bad dudes. One was an escapee from a federal prison for bank robbery, and the other one was out of Texas, wanted for murder. They had peeled the safe at the Arbor Inn restaurant, just south of the canal on Central Avenue, then they drove along the canal bank to 7th Street where you jumped them. The rest of you guys could take a lesson from this rookie. Keep your eyes open and your head out of your ass and no telling what you might run across."

Luke wished his sergeant would get off the subject. He didn't like being the center of attention. He just wanted to keep a low profile and complete his probation.

"By the way, I have some commendations here. The rest of you involved in the chase did an excellent job." Sergeant Richards handed written commendations to Officer Creech and several others.

"You did a good job, Canfield," Richards said before heading for the lieutenant's office, "but probationers don't get written commendations."

That was fine with Luke. He didn't need the acknowledgment. He was just happy that everything turned out all right. At least he had a decent line for his worksheet.

CHAPTER FIVE

A week had passed since his running gun battle, and for the past two days, Luke had been riding solo and assigned to a regular beat. The word of how well he'd handled such a dangerous situation, and the fact that his alertness had put some bad guys in jail, had a positive influence on the way he was treated. No one called him rookie any longer. Even Dennis Creech treated him as just another member of the squad.

It was still difficult to find something that would justify a line on his worksheet. He stopped a few traffic violators and wrote some tickets, but ticket writing wasn't something he liked to do. All he could think about was how much it was going to cost the driver. He knew first-hand how difficult it was to come up with the money for an unexpected expense.

There had been a rash of high dollar burglaries in the Sunnyslope area recently. A safe was peeled on two occasions and blown open on another. Hardly any criminals used nitro anymore. It was unstable and too dangerous. It took a real pro to successfully blow a safe.

Sergeant Richards voiced his concern one night at briefing. "We're having too damn many burglaries in our area," he bellowed. "The lieutenant is on my ass, and since shit rolls downhill, I'm going to be on your asses until you catch the sonsabitches who are breaking into these places. They're going through the roof on some of these, so keep an eye out for anyone carrying a ladder. That shouldn't be too hard to spot."

The sergeant thumbed through his notebook. "Most of you probably know Jimmy Granger, the last of the nitro men. He's a sociable asshole and he might have even bought some of you a cup of coffee from time to time. I've drank coffee with him. Seems he likes cops; at least when he's not blowing safes. It's a pretty sure bet he's the one who blew the safe at Hilda's Jewelers a week ago. He has a heart condition and I suspect we'll eventually find him in front of a safe, dead from a heart attack. But I don't wanta wait that long. Catch the son of a bitch."

The sergeant started for the lieutenant's office, but suddenly turned back. "Canfield, you haven't performed any heroics for over a week. So maybe you can stumble onto one of these assholes like you did on the two that knocked over the restaurant on the canal. Just try not to get another car shot full of holes."

"Yeah, Rook." Creech echoed. "Go out and catch these guys, but watch out they don't catch you. They might be a better shot next time."

Luke felt his blood pressure rise. No one had called him rookie in a long time. Now Dennis Creech had started it up again. It was best not to reply. He ignored the comment and continued taking notes from the Blue Book.

Three suspects had robbed a bank in Michigan and another in Colorado. Authorities had received information they were headed for California.

They weren't likely to pass through Phoenix, but Luke jotted down the description and license plate number of the car they were driving. It gave him something to do so he wouldn't dwell too much on his dislike for fellow officer Creech. It also made him look busy and interested in his job in case his sergeant was watching.

***

Two months on night shift was nearly over. A few more days and all uniformed patrol officers would change to shift two. Luke liked working the afternoon shift. It was a lot busier and time went faster. The only drawback was not being home with his family in the evenings.

After briefing, he pulled out of the station parking lot and followed his usual swing south on 7th Street. The big Ford police car he was driving was a lot more powerful than the Studebaker Lark that got shot up on his first night solo. Luke was happy with the upgrade. He figured it was a perk for making his sergeant look good during the chase, since there were no injuries and the suspects were captured. He'd heard that Sergeant Richards had received a commendation for taking charge of the situation which culminated in the arrest of two suspects and the clearance of several safe burglaries.

Luke noticed two cars parked in front of the donut shop as he passed. The building's large front windows permitted a clear view inside. A man and a woman sat at the far end of the counter. Another man stood waiting by the takeout area.

He slowed as he came to the canal where he'd jumped the two guys who shot at him. He guessed he'd never pass that location again without thinking how close he came to getting his head blown off. He still couldn't figure out what had stopped him from walking up to that car. It was like he had hit an invisible wall; not only once, but twice.

Something, or someone, had kept him from getting killed. Not only when he tried approaching the car, but also while searching for the man who was lying in wait behind a bush near the crash scene. How could that be? It didn't make any sense. He wracked his brain, but there was no rational explanation. He finally gave up and tried not to think about it. But he couldn't entirely dismiss it from his mind. Since that day in the barn at the age of nine, a voice in his head kept reminding him he was different.

Luke loved the farm and all that it represented. His heart and soul were there. Throughout his youth, he couldn't imagine ever doing anything else. But with maturity came complications. Things that seemed to be etched in stone turned out to be fragile tales of past events; like something written in the dust and blown away with a single gust of wind. Fate was the determining factor.

Luke shook off his ruminations. He couldn't let his mind become too absorbed with the past. He needed a clear head. Police officers who became too distracted wound up dead.

After passing the Arizona Canal, Luke continued south on 7th Street to Northern, east to 12th Street, then north.

He was nearly back to Dunlap when he suddenly got

the urge to check out the vehicles he'd seen at the donut shop. Everything had looked all right when he passed, but something didn't feel right.

A swing west on Dunlap to 7th Street, then south to the donut shop, left him feeling a little apprehensive about running into a similar situation as his first night solo. Emily would really throw a fit if he got shot at again.

The same couple he'd seen earlier were still seated at the counter. But the man waiting for takeout was gone. So was his vehicle.

Luke breathed a sigh of relief. "There I go again, getting all worked up for nothing," he muttered as he drove slowly past. He would stop in later and get his usual cup of coffee and donut, but for now, he'd better find something to put on his worksheet. Sergeant Richards might let him slide a week or two after his run-in with the burglary suspects who shot at him, but his grace period wouldn't last long.

He checked some businesses to make sure the doors and windows were intact, stopped by the donut shop for coffee, and headed north on 7th Street to Dunlap, where a veer to the right put him northbound on Cave Creek Road.

Phoenix was laid out with nearly every major street running north and south or east and west clear across the valley.

Only two cut diagonally: Grand Avenue on the west side and Cave Creek Road in the northeast.

Luke fell in behind a green Mercury, but the driver was obeying all traffic laws. There was no evidence to show this was a possible drunk driver. He turned onto a side street and swung back towards Hatcher. Still, there was something about that car with out of state plates. He wished he'd have gotten the license number, but all he recalled was that it was from Michigan.

He pulled to the curb and thumbed hurriedly through his notes. Buried deep in the pile was the information he'd copied at briefing more than a month earlier. Only because Dennis Creech had gotten under Luke's skin and Luke wanted to look busy in front of his sergeant.

After careful scrutiny, Luke managed to decipher his scribbling: Three bank robbery suspects in a green Mercury with Michigan plates. He hadn't noticed the license plate, but one of the cars he'd seen in front of the donut shop at the beginning of his shift was a green Mercury. It was too much of a coincidence not to be the same vehicle he'd just followed.

The more Luke thought about it, the more convinced he was that it was also the car listed in the Blue-Book; the one the three bank robbers were driving.

He picked up the mic, but slowly replaced it. What was

he going to say? That he *thinks* he might have spotted the bank robber's car? Then why did he wait half the shift to report it? And if he just saw it again, why didn't he stop it? Was he scared of being shot at again?

Worse yet, what if it turned out to be the wrong car and he got everyone all worked up over nothing. He imagined all sorts of derogatory comments, especially from Dennis Creech. No, he would just have to locate the car and either eliminate it or make sure it was the one they were looking for.

If the vehicle was still on the street, he should be able to find it. But after a thorough search with no success, he decided he was probably making something out of nothing. His time would be better spent trying to find a line for his worksheet.

Several bars strung out along Cave Creek Road were usually the source of "hot calls," especially on Friday and Saturday nights. But it was Monday, and everything was quiet.

A quick glance at a cluster of businesses just south of Mountain View Road revealed nothing out of the ordinary. But Luke got a strange feeling as he slowly passed.

He spotted a car in the parking lot of a pawn shop. It was a green Mercury backed against the block wall. The front license plate was missing.

Since there was nobody in the vehicle, Luke's first thought

was that someone had pawned it and pulled the plates. But it was the same make and color as the one he was looking for. He decided to check it out.

He whipped a U-turn and shut off his headlights before coasting to a stop near the corner of the building. Slowly and quietly he slid out of his car, careful not to slam the door.

With flashlight at the ready and his hand on his gun, Luke rounded the corner of the building.

It took a minute to adjust his eyes to the dimly lit area, but Luke could see three figures huddled around the back door of the pawn shop. One of them appeared to be trying to pry the door open. He pulled his gun and switched on his flashlight.

"Don't anyone move," Luke yelled as he stepped closer. "Drop the tool and get your hands up."

The three men turned to face him, but remained motionless, their hands at their sides. One still held the crowbar he'd been using to pry the door.

"I said drop that tool and get your hands up," Luke repeated.

The suspects remained still.

I shoulda thoughts filled Luke's mind. *I shoulda backed off and called for a backup. I shoulda driven back here so I would be close to my radio. I shoulda...*

What the hell was he going to do now? He couldn't just shoot them if they weren't an immediate threat. He didn't know how long this stalemate would continue. He had to do something.

He started to back away. Maybe he could get to his car and ask for a backup before the suspects could scatter too far; especially since he was between them and their car. But when he stepped back, they stepped forward.

He considered firing a warning shot next to their feet, but quickly discounted that idea. Warning shots were prohibited by policy and he was still on probation. It could be enough to get him fired.

Luke took another step back, but the suspects were moving forward at a faster pace than he was retreating.

He cocked his revolver. He'd had enough backing up. He took a step forward, his voice calm. "You with the crowbar, drop it or I'll put a bullet in you. And you other two are next."

A car suddenly tore around the corner of the building, its headlights on bright. Flashing red lights immediately followed. Luke breathed a sigh of relief. It was a patrol car.

"Hey assholes, get your mangy asses down on the ground or I'll put 'em down permanently." Officer Dennis Creech had come to the rescue.

The man with the crowbar dropped the tool and all three

slowly lowered themselves to the ground just as two more police cars barreled in from the opposite direction.

Luke suspected Creech must have had presence of mind to immediately analyze the situation and call for backup. Something Luke should have done. Maybe he deserved to be called a rookie. After all, he did make a dumb mistake that put him in danger of being killed or him killing one or more of the suspects.

After the suspects were cuffed and placed in separate patrol cars, Luke approached the officer who had just bailed him out of a sticky situation.

"Thanks for the help, Dennis. They weren't following my commands and I was afraid I was going to have to shoot them."

"I doubt they had anything to worry about," Creech smirked. "There were three of them and your gun only holds six bullets."

In another setting, Luke would have been miffed at the snide remark, but not here, not now. "You're probably right," he replied with a grin.

Another police car pulled in. Sergeant Richards.

"What the hell were you doing back here, Canfield?" he growled. "You trying to get yourself killed just to make me look bad?"

He examined the back door of the pawn shop that had

obviously been jimmied.

"All you got is an attempted burglary. That won't keep them tied up for very long. How did you run onto them?"

"Well, I saw a Mercury in the parking lot. It didn't have a plate on the front and I couldn't see the one on the back. It fit the description of one used in some bank robberies so I decided to check it out. I'll check the plate to see if it's the same vehicle."

Luke quickly walked to the Mercury before his sergeant could grill him any further. He crawled over the trunk and checked the plate. It matched the one he had in his notes.

"It's the same car," he said. "They've been knocking off banks clear across the country. I saw the information in the Blue Book about a month ago."

"If they've been pulling bank robberies, why the hell would they bother trying to break into a pawn shop? That doesn't make any sense," Creech quipped.

"They probably needed more guns. A pawnshop is a perfect place to get some without causing too much attention," Richards countered.

He gave Luke a skeptical look. "You saw the information in the Blue Book a month ago and remembered it?"

"I just remembered it was a Mercury with Michigan plates," Luke explained. He tried to downplay the incident in order to get Richards off his ass.

He wanted to tell his sergeant that Dennis Creech had saved the day. Otherwise he would have been forced to shoot one or more of the suspects. But that would be admitting he had screwed up by not advising radio of his location and asking for a backup before he confronted the suspects. After all, he was still a probationer. Any screw-up that serious could get him fired. No, he would just keep his mouth shut and thank Creech in private.

"If it hadn't been for Dennis, I would probably have had to shoot one or more of them. I got the drop on them and ordered them to put up their hands and stay where they were, but they refused to do it and started advancing towards me. Dennis came just in time." Luke had no intention of saying anything like that. But the words came tumbling out. He'd better get ready for whatever his sergeant decided to do.

Sergeant Richards shifted his glance back and forth between his two subordinates before responding.

"Well, it was a good thing he showed up then, wasn't it? Let this be a lesson to both of you. When you hear another officer go Code-6, swing by and see if everything is OK. Good job, Creech." Sergeant Richards returned to his car and left the parking lot.

After everyone had gone, Luke asked dispatch for a tow

truck. He would inventory the suspect's vehicle while waiting.

He glanced around the deserted parking lot that a few minutes earlier was a chaotic scene of police cars and flashing red lights. If it hadn't been for Dennis Creech, a guy who was normally a pain in the ass, Luke might have had to shoot someone or been killed himself.

Creech never even mentioned to Sergeant Richards that the rookie had failed to follow department policy by not advising radio of his location and situation. No telling what might have happened if he had. There might have been one less probationer on his squad. Funny how situations and beliefs that seem to be etched in stone can change so rapidly into something else.

A sudden sadness engulfed him. Memories of his little sister came flooding back. If only he had paid more attention to detail. If only he had made sure the gate was latched before running to the barn. If only...

"Too late now," he sighed as he pushed the thoughts aside and began the inventory process. "It's too late now."

CHAPTER SIX

The days passed without further incident. Shift two changed to shift one. It was another blistering-hot day, and even though it was only a little after 10 a.m., Luke's uniform shirt was already soaked with sweat. None of the older police cars were equipped with air conditioning and he was unlucky enough to have drawn one of the oldest.

The accident report he'd just completed was also wet from sweat that had dripped off him while trying to write. Most officers completed the more complicated and lengthy reports while on break in a restaurant. But along with a shitty car, Luke also drew a beat on the outer fringe of the city that he seemed to get more often than anyone else. Area wise, Six-ten was one of the largest beats in the entire city. But it had more cactus, rattle snakes, and scorpions than it did people. He didn't mind. It was worth braving the relentless sun in the daytime, if he could prowl around the desert at night.

Unlike most who complained about having to patrol a "wasteland," Luke found the desert to be a marvel of ever changing personalities.

In the daytime, the area was a hot and dusty expanse of quiet solitude without a creature stirring. As the day wore on and the shadows lengthened, it began to take on a more complicated look with a promise of mystery. But at night, it was as if the darkness had opened up a door to another world.

Saguaro cactus, silhouetted in the moonlight, could easily be mistaken for grotesque giants with outstretched arms waiting to gather you in if you dared to get too close. And after a rain, the desert would come alive with a magical transformation of sights, sounds, and smells that seemed to transcend the bounds of time and space.

The scurry of a rabbit, the yap of a coyote, the grunt and snort of a javelina, and the occasional screech of an owl seemed to herald the meager drops of rain to this parched piece of land.

Luke would often sit quietly with the car windows down and take in the unmistakable fragrance of lavender, sage, and creosote that wafted through the night air. If he had to work nights, beat Six-ten was the one to have.

But it hadn't been that long ago since he'd rotated to day shift, and it hadn't rained in months. Several small dust-devils, waltzing their way across a bare patch of ground, made everything look even drier. They reminded Luke that he needed a cup of coffee.

The closest restaurant was way off his beat. He decided to head that way. The dispatcher, however, interrupted his plans.

"Six-ten?" It was a pleasant voice with a no-nonsense attitude.

"Six-ten," Luke answered.

"Six-ten, see the complainant at…She really couldn't give an exact address. She hasn't lived there very long. She said it was an old house that sits by itself in the middle of a cotton field near 43rd Avenue and Thunderbird."

"Did she say what the problem was?" Luke asked.

"I don't have that information," came the reply.

Someone must have stolen some of her cotton, Luke mused as he headed to the call. *I hope she has air conditioning.*

"How in the hell am I supposed to get there?" he griped loudly to himself as he spied the house, but was stymied by the rows of cotton that surrounded it.

After a short search, he discovered a dirt road that ran

alongside an irrigation ditch. He guided the police car over the bumpy trail and pulled up under a large cottonwood tree near the house.

It was still hotter than hell. But the shade offered some relief from the searing sun. He picked up his clipboard, pulled some report forms out of the metal box that all officers carried, and reluctantly left the shady tree.

"Damn. This place must be a hundred years old," he muttered as he took inventory of the weathered siding and missing shingles on his way to the door. "Guess I can forget about any air conditioning here."

The inner door was closed and the metal screen door was warped and sat at an odd angle, leaving a gap between the leading edge and the door frame. The foot plate was intact, but most of the screen was missing.

He banged on the screen door, creating a rattling sound that threatened to tear it from its worn-out hinges.

After waiting a reasonable amount of time without anyone coming to the door, Luke banged harder. It was too damned hot to stand around in the boiling sun waiting for someone to answer.

As he was about to return to his car to get further information from the dispatcher, a woman's head emerged from an open window. "Be careful officer," she cautioned. "That snake is right there by your feet."

Luke glanced down to see a large snake coiled between the inner door and the base plate of the screen door. It was black with white bands.

He immediately froze. Snakes scared the hell out of him, no matter what kind they were. But this one looked deadlier than any he'd ever seen. Anything that looked that scary had to be poisonous. Was this the way he was supposed to die? Not as a hero in a blazing gun battle felled by the bullet of a hardened criminal, but by a venomous snake in the middle of a cotton field? What had he done to deserve a fate such as this?

He tried to turn his head so he wouldn't have to witness the death dealing fangs sink into his flesh and deliver their lethal dose of poison. But his body failed to respond. He couldn't keep from staring and he couldn't turn his head. It was as if the snake had some evil hypnotic power that prevented him from moving or thinking rationally.

A stinging pain in his eyes from the sweat rolling down his forehead seemed to break the spell. Slowly, he backed away and with shaky legs, returned to his car.

He slid onto the seat, his hands clasped tightly around the steering wheel. His heart pounded and his uniform was drenched with sweat, not only from the heat, but terror driven sweat; the clammy kind normally experienced as the result of a nightmare. The snake, however, was a living, breathing, fully awake nightmare. They didn't get any scarier than that.

As soon as Luke regained sufficient composure to speak without his voice trembling, he keyed the mic and asked radio to send Animal Control. He didn't know if the snake was poisonous and he didn't really give a damn. Let the professionals, the snake charmers, deal with the damned thing.

After what seemed like half a day, Animal Control showed up and corralled the snake. They chastised the officer for calling them out for a non-poisonous king snake. But as far as Luke was concerned, a snake was a snake. He didn't care what their title was.

***

Luke had less than a month left on his probation. For the past several weeks he'd been assigned to the paddy wagon, a converted bread truck used to transport prisoners from the field to the jail downtown.

Since there was room in the wagon for at least eight people–more if you crammed them in–beat cops turned their prisoners and accompanying paperwork over to the wagon officers. It was the responsibility of the wagon officers to deliver the prisoners and booking slips to the jail, and related paperwork to the front desk at the main police station.

Luke's wagon partner was a senior officer who had recently transferred from South Side.

Bill Blasset was a likeable guy, always cheerful and easy going, except when the conversation involved his twelve-year-old daughter, a constant runaway. He would then become dark and brooding.

"We've done everything for that girl," he groused. "She still refuses to obey. I even bought her a bicycle, thinking that would make her happy. But it seems no matter what we do, it's never enough."

Luke offered sympathy, but he couldn't think of anything to say that would make his partner feel better. He couldn't imagine how devastating it would be if one of his kids ran away.

During one of his darker days, shortly after his daughter was returned home after running away once again, Blasset turned to Luke with a helpless expression.

"I'd better swing by the house and make sure my daughter is still there. Short of locking her in her room, I don't know what to do," he said.

"Sure. No problem," Luke replied.

While still several blocks away, Blasset quietly asked, "Would you mind talking to her? Maybe you can get through to her that she needs to do what I say, at least until she's eighteen."

Luke was surprised and flattered that a senior officer would ask a rookie to talk his daughter out of running away from home. What the hell did Luke know about such things? He hadn't been on the department long enough to know anything.

"Be glad to," he replied.

As they pulled up to the Blasset residence, Luke still had no idea what he was going to say to a twelve-year-old girl that her father hadn't already tried. He was still trying to come up with something as they entered the house.

Sara Blasset was a skinny little girl with long golden hair that cascaded over her shoulders like a waterfall. It made her appear older than she actually was. She never looked up as the men entered the room. Her attention was riveted to the television.

"Hello, young lady. Why aren't you in school?" Luke asked in his most official sounding tone.

Sara glanced quickly at the officer before sullenly turning her attention back to cartoons.

Her father switched off the television. "Officer Canfield wants to talk to you. The least you can do is listen to what he has to say."

Sara remained silent and unmoving, still staring at the darkened screen of the television.

"I'll be in the kitchen," her father said. "It might be better if you talk with her alone."

He clasped Luke on the shoulder before leaving the room.

Luke moved to a point near the television where he could face the young girl who was causing his partner so much grief. What was he going to say that would set her on the right path? He didn't have a clue.

"Don't you like school?" he asked.

She didn't answer.

"I didn't like school either when I first started," Luke quipped. "I was born and raised on a farm and there were too many fun things I would rather do than go to school. So I used to run away, too."

Sara sat motionless and continued to ignore him.

"Do you know where I ran to? I didn't go very far. I always hid in the same place–the outhouse. But my older sister always found me and made me go to school anyway." Luke chuckled. "You'd think I'd wise up after the first dozen times and hide somewhere else, but..."

The young girl shifted her attention from the blank television screen, and for the first time, looked directly at the officer. It was a hollow stare; a look that belied her tender age. The down and out, the homeless and the hopeless all had stares like that. Still, she said nothing.

Luke felt a chill. What had this girl, his partner's daughter, experienced in her young life that would create such an empty look? Maybe something had happened during one of her ventures away from home that scarred her emotionally and she was too traumatized to explain it.

"You know you can talk to me about anything," Luke said as Sara shifted her gaze back to the blank television. "I have kids too. Two girls and a boy. Sometimes they have bad days, but we always talk them out. I'm really not much of a talker, but I'm a good listener if there's anything you want to talk about."

Sara turned her head and eyed him intently. "I don't want to live here anymore," she said softly. "I want to live somewhere else."

Luke was overwhelmed by a strange sense of sadness. His eyes began to water. What the hell was going on? He needed to get hold of himself and concentrate on helping his partner convince this young girl not to run away. "I think we all want to get away sometimes," he said. "But you know you have to do what your parents tell you until you're eighteen. Then you can do whatever you want and go wherever you want. Time goes fast.

You'll be eighteen before you know it."

"We'd better go," Blasset said. "We've been away from the radio too long. We'll stop by later."

Luke looked up to find his partner standing in the doorway. He must have been there all along, listening to what was said. It was understandable. After all, it was his daughter, and he couldn't entirely trust what a rookie might say.

Luke had forgotten about the possibility of getting a radio call. He had focused his full attention on Sara Blasset. Too bad they had to leave just when he might be getting somewhere. Maybe they could swing by on their lunch break when they had more time.

The call of a combative prisoner directed Luke's thoughts to the situation they were about to face. The issue with his partner's daughter would have to wait.

Over the next month, Luke tried unsuccessfully to return to the Blasset home for a further attempt to talk with Sara. It seemed they were always too busy.

***

It was mid-morning on a Friday when the wagon received a call to report to the office of Field Operations.

"Wonder what they want?" Luke gave his partner a questioning glance. "My probation is nearly up. Maybe they think I'm not cut out for this job and want to hire someone who is."

"Nothing to get concerned about. Probably just another detail," Blasset replied. "They probably want us to run an errand or transport something. That's one bad thing about working the wagon. You always get the shit details."

Luke had been to the main station on numerous occasions when he had to drop off booking material or pick up something from the front desk. But he had never been in the division office.

It was a bustling place with the Division Commander's office at one end and secretary work stations scattered throughout the room. The Administrative Sergeant's desk fronted the main entrance.

A large personnel board on the wall behind the sergeant's desk held magnetic name tags in a variety of colors of everyone assigned to the division. It was an impressive sight.

"Come with me," the desk sergeant said as he headed to a back room.

Both officers turned to follow. The sergeant looked at Luke and pointed to a bench along the wall. "Not you. You have a seat over there."

Luke took a seat. "Guess I'm not important enough to be

in on whatever it is they want done," he muttered as he watched his partner disappear into the back room.

At least they didn't call us in to fire me. The thought raised his spirits until another thought took its place. *Maybe they're asking my partner what he thinks about my performance before they make up their minds.*

After a few minutes, the desk sergeant emerged from the back room.

Luke held his breath, waiting for the sergeant to tell him whether or not he would remain on the job. But the sergeant took his seat and resumed working on some papers stacked in front of him.

Ten minutes went by. Then twenty. Luke was getting nervous. If they weren't discussing him, then what? He couldn't imagine any detail that would take such a long briefing. He wanted to ask the sergeant what was going on, but the man had been completely ignoring him. It was best to keep his mouth shut.

"What's taking so long?" The words slipped out before Luke could call them back.

The desk sergeant briefly looked up from his paperwork. "I dunno. Just sit tight."

In order to kill time, Luke carefully examined the personnel board behind the sergeants' desk, looking for his name.

Most of the names were blue, while others were black, green, white, and purple. He finally located his name. But why was it in green? Further inspection revealed a number of green name tags across the board. His entire academy class was labeled in green. He calmed down after determining blue must be the designated color for all uniformed patrol officers. Green were those still on probation. He surmised that the other colors must designate special operations personnel and clerical staff.

How the hell could anyone keep track of so many people and keep that board up to date? That alone would take all day.

He watched as the sergeant examined each piece of paper from a huge stack before placing it in one of several baskets on his desk. It seemed to Luke like an overwhelming task. He shook his head as he wondered who the hell could stand being cooped up in an office all day shuffling papers. It was a nightmare thought.

An hour went by, and still no word from his partner or an explanation from the sergeant.

Then, a door slowly opened in the back room and Bill Blasset emerged in handcuffs flanked by two detectives. His uniform shirt was missing, exposing a white T-shirt.

Luke thought he was seeing things. *What the hell was his partner doing in handcuffs?* He stood speechless as the trio brushed past him and out the door.

"What's going on?" Luke asked the desk sergeant. "Why is my partner in cuffs? What did he do? Should I still wait for him?"

"No, you can go," the sergeant replied. "Since you're riding a two-man unit, you'd better return to your briefing station and report to your sergeant."

Luke hurried to the briefing station where Sergeant Richards was waiting, along with one of his squad members.

"Bobby Hill will be your partner for the rest of the shift," Richards announced.

"Where is Blasset? Why was he arrested?" Luke asked.

"I don't have any information on that yet," Richards replied. "Maybe tomorrow. You two hit the street."

Luke reluctantly left the station with his new partner and climbed into the passenger side. He handed his partner the keys. "You'll have to drive," he said. "I'm still too shook up. What the hell would they arrest my partner for? Like he doesn't have enough trouble with his daughter running away all the time?"

He wondered what Blasset could have done. The vision of a fellow officer in handcuffs and stripped of his uniform shirt was heavy on Luke's mind. They hadn't ridden together very long, but Luke thought he knew everything about the man.

***

The following day, Sergeant Richards made an announcement. "We'll be one short until we get a replacement. Seems *Ex*-Officer Bill Blasset was molesting his daughter. She got tired of running away from home and finally told the officer who picked her up all about it. Apparently, it had been going on for years. The son of a bitch should have been castrated and hung, instead of fired and booked."

Everyone sat motionless. It was as though time had stopped. Even Dennis Creech, who always had something caustic to say, remained silent.

Luke was shocked. How could his partner, an officer sworn to uphold the law, commit such a vile act? Maybe there was some mistake. Maybe the girl was making up the story in an attempt to justify her running away. Maybe...

No. There were no maybes. He would just have to accept the facts. The person he liked, respected, and sympathized with was a child molester. And Luke thought he knew him.

Does anyone ever really know anybody?

CHAPTER SEVEN

With little fanfare, Luke's probationary period was up and he was presented with his final monthly performance rating.

He grinned when he saw the box marked "Acceptable Performance." It was a relief not to have to worry about his employment being terminated on the whim of a supervisor. He'd been fortunate to have Bill Richards as his probationary sergeant.

Except when he was on the 3 to 11 shift, most evenings were spent around the supper table discussing the kid's activities. On his days off, the family would occasionally eat out. Luke would rather have spent every evening at home, but Emily and the kids liked the restaurant adventure so he never balked.

Although his days off sometimes changed, they were always weekdays. Probationers and junior officers were seldom

afforded weekends. Those were reserved for the more senior. Luke
didn't mind. In fact, he preferred Tuesdays and Wednesdays off.
That meant fewer people to contend with at restaurants and other
places the family went.

The kids–Rebecca 9, Michael 6, and Amy 5–were barely
big enough to peer above the table, but they were well behaved.
With a little help from their parents, they selected menu items
and placed orders to share. They especially liked the heavenly
drumsticks and the egg foo yung at Chung's Chinese restaurant.

Luke smiled as the memory of one eventful night
highlighted Emily's amazing ability to turn an embarrassing
situation into something positive, especially when it involved the
children.

They had ordered their food and were discussing school
activities when, Michael, in his enthusiasm to explain how he
was able to elude a fellow classmate in a game of tag, accidentally
knocked over his water. He sat wide-eyed and speechless as Luke
grabbed some napkins and soaked up what he could.

"Oh, oh," Amy said. "Michael spilled. It's all wet." She
gingerly held up a soggy napkin that was dripping water.

Michael made a half-hearted attempt to help, his head
hanging in shame.

Without saying a word, Emily quickly drank most of the

water from her glass and as she set it down, she deliberately tipped it over, adding to the mess already there.

"Gee, Michael, I guess you and I are water-tippers tonight," she chuckled. "We must be related. That just goes to show that we all sometimes have little accidents, even big people."

Michael beamed as he helped mop up and resumed his story.

Luke smiled and gave his wife an approving look. While he wouldn't have scolded his son for the accident, neither would he have thought to immediately relieve Michael of the embarrassment by knocking over his own water.

It was the little things she did that kept Luke falling in love with his wife over and over again. He couldn't imagine it would ever be any other way.

CHAPTER EIGHT

A year had passed since Luke completed his probationary period, and a number of personnel changes were in the works. Sergeant Richards was being transferred to the detective bureau, along with Dennis Creech.

Since the squad was working day shift and the transfers were effective the following Monday, a party was being held at the Richards residence on Saturday night to celebrate the occasion. The entire squad, along with their wives, was invited to attend.

Luke doubted Emily would go. She had previously accompanied him to several police functions and she complained for weeks afterwards. "They talk about nothing but police work. I'm left out of the conversation. I feel like a fifth wheel."

Luke felt obligated to attend. After all, it was Sergeant

Richards' last chance to socialize with his squad. If Emily refused to go, he would go alone.

"My sergeant is being transferred to detectives and he's having a squad party to celebrate," Luke explained. "Everyone is expected to attend, including the wives. He's been a good supervisor. I think we should go." He braced himself for her negative response.

"Yes, I think we should," Emily replied.

Luke couldn't believe his ears. He didn't even have to talk her into it. But this was only Monday. She still had nearly a week to change her mind.

It wasn't until Saturday night when they were on the way that Luke breathed a sigh of relief. Emily wasn't thrilled about going, he knew that. She had agreed to go just to please him.

The party was in full swing when they pulled up to the Richards residence, a modest slump-block house a few blocks south of the Sunnyslope briefing station.

Sylvia Richards was an attractive woman, with long red hair that curled up at the ends. Freckles, splattered across her face and neck, provided a complimentary accent. Luke had met her at a previous function and found her to be gracious and charming.

"Hello," Sylvia said as she ushered her guests inside. "Glad you could make it."

"Thanks for the invite," Luke replied.

He and Emily followed their host into the kitchen where all nine members of his squad were present, except for Dennis Creech.

"Maybe this won't be such a bad party after all," Luke muttered. "At least Mr. Smart Ass isn't here."

After the usual greetings and introduction of Emily to the group, Luke fished a Coors from the ice chest and handed Emily a coke. He would have preferred a cup of coffee, but he didn't see anything other than soft drinks and beer.

After escorting Emily into the living room where most of the women were admiring some ceramics that Mrs. Richards had made, he returned to the kitchen. It was an old habit from his days on the farm. The kitchen was where most informal visiting took place. It was also closest to the food.

Luke picked up two paper plates and some hors d'oeuvres and took one in to Emily, who was deep in conversation with a man. Luke was surprised to see her laughing and appearing to have a good time. He was even further surprised to see who she'd found to be so interesting: Dennis Creech.

Guess I counted my chickens before they hatched. That guy keeps turning up like a bad dream.

The thought remained even as Luke handed his wife the

plate of snacks and acknowledged Creech's presence.

"Hi Dennis," Luke said. "Where did you come from? I was just in here and didn't see you anywhere around. Did you bring your wife?"

"And you're a trained observer?" Creech smirked. "I was just talking with your lovely wife. She's intelligent, too. I'm going to have to come to these parties more often." The question about bringing his wife went unanswered.

Emily flashed a broad smile as she thanked her husband for the food. "Dennis and I were just talking about the latest fashion trends. It's refreshing to speak with someone who is capable of discussing something other than police activity. Are you sure he's a cop?"

"That's debatable," Luke answered with a smirk of his own before turning back to the kitchen.

Even though it irritated the hell out of him to see his wife cozying up to a guy who was a constant pain in the ass, it was the first time he'd seen her enjoy being at a squad party and he wasn't about to put a damper on it.

On the ride home, Emily mentioned the good time she'd had at the party and how interesting Dennis was.

"He is very intellectual," she said. "He has a brilliant mind. He knows art. He knows fashion. He knows literature. No matter what I brought up, he was knowledgeable about it. We have similar tastes. He even thought the same cartoons that I'd found to be so hilarious in the New Yorker were funny. How did a man like that ever become a police officer?"

"I've asked myself that same question," Luke answered.

The following day as Emily was preparing supper, she mentioned again how much she enjoyed talking with Dennis Creech.

Luke poured himself a cup of coffee, dumped in some milk, and took a swallow. "Yeah, well. Did you notice that he never answered my question about his wife?" he quipped. "If he has one, no one has ever seen her. Maybe he keeps her locked up somewhere. Or maybe he's too obnoxious to get a woman to spend more than five minutes with him, let alone marry him."

"Do I detect a note of jealousy?" Emily teased.

"Are you kidding?" Luke hastily replied. "Of him?"

He set his coffee down and gathered his wife in his arms. "Well, maybe a little." He grinned as he kissed her lightly. "Maybe a little."

CHAPTER NINE

Sergeant Richard's replacement was a much younger man. Dave Hastings had come out number one on the sergeant's promotional list on his first attempt. He made no secret about his desire to rise to higher rank as quickly as possible, and he expected his subordinates to help him get there.

Hastings' main interest was traffic enforcement. He let it be known during briefing on his first day.

"There's no reason why every one of you can't bring in at least a half-dozen tickets a day. There are traffic violators all over the place. So when you're not on a call, I expect you to be shagging traffic signals and other hot spots and writing some tickets."

Luke grimaced. Writing tickets was something he disliked

the most about his job. He realized the importance of traffic enforcement, and he understood it was part of his job. But catching robbers, burglars, and other bad guys seemed more important, and it was a hell of a lot more interesting. He'd always held the opinion that guys who liked writing tickets were on some kind of power trip that seemed to make up for their deep seated feeling of inferiority. Sergeant Hastings appeared to be a prime example.

What can't be cured must be endured. Luke had often used that mantra to get him through some tough times. He would have to rely on it once again.

Six weeks after Hastings had taken over the squad, Luke was called into the sergeant's office.

"Canfield," the sergeant said. "I've been looking over your stats. You've done a good job catching criminals and recovering stolen vehicles. But there's more to police work than enforcing criminal laws. Traffic laws must be equally enforced. From going over your personnel file, I see on your first night solo you stopped a car for a traffic related offense which ultimately resulted in the capture of two felons. Criminals need cars to get around. So don't disregard a part of the job that you find less interesting for something more glamorous."

Never skip over something important because you're anxious about something else. The words of his sergeant, as well as his tone of voice, triggered the admonishment Luke's father had given him that day in the barn so many years ago.

He rubbed his hand across his face as he came out of his flashback. His sergeant's words were starting to fully register again.

"Some people feel it's beneath them to enforce traffic laws. They see no glory in it. But we are not in a position to be selective. It is our sworn duty to enforce all the laws. You've been averaging less than two traffic citations per day. I wrote more than that on my first day out of the academy."

"Yes, of course, Sarge," Luke said. "I agree we need to enforce traffic laws. But I just haven't seen that many violations that would justify a ticket. I'll concentrate more on traffic."

Hastings closed his stat-book and set it aside. "I think you'll probably be more productive assigned to the wagon. That way, you won't be expected to write many tickets and it will free up an officer who is more traffic oriented."

Luke breathed a sigh of relief. He liked riding the wagon. Unlike a beat car, the wagon could go anywhere in the squad area. And since it was always a two-man unit, it was called to all major incidents. One drawback, however, was family-fight calls. They usually fell to the wagon.

Luke began his wagon assignment the following day with

a rookie partner. It hadn't been that long ago since he'd been designated that title. He made up his mind not to treat his junior partner the way Dennis Creech had treated him.

Sergeant Hastings introduced him. "This is Gary Styles. He'll be your wagon partner. He tells me traffic enforcement is something he's interested in, so maybe some of his enthusiasm will rub off on you."

"Welcome aboard." Luke extended his hand.

Gary Styles was a quiet, bespectacled twenty-three-year-old. His slim build and withdrawn nature was more in line with a bookkeeper than a cop. The wire-rimmed glasses he wore reinforced that appearance.

"Tell me about yourself," Luke said as they wound their way out of the busy parking lot and onto Dunlap Avenue.

"I don't think that car came to a full stop at the stop sign," Styles said as they proceeded west towards Central Avenue. "Didn't you see him?" He swiveled his head in an attempt to visually follow the violator headed in the opposite direction.

"It looked like he'd stopped to me," Luke countered. "Some people stop a ways back from the stop sign and then proceed through. If you weren't watching their approach, it would look like they hadn't stopped. You have to be careful with that."

"Sergeant Hastings likes to see lots of traffic enforcement. I believe that would have been a good ticket," the rookie said.

"When in doubt, strike it out." Luke repeated the phrase his training officer, Fred Sloan, had often used to justify not writing a ticket. "You've heard it said that it's better to let a hundred guilty go free than to hang one innocent man? Well, I feel the same about traffic tickets. It would be wise for you to adopt the same philosophy. It doesn't take long to develop a reputation for writing shitty tickets. And that is something you'll never recover from. So make sure it's a clear violation before breaking out your ticket book."

"Wagon 61," the radio crackled.

When his partner failed to pick up the mic, Luke grabbed it.

"Wagon 61."

"Wagon 61, Six-eleven is requesting a wagon for a combative prisoner at 16839 North 17th Place."

"10-4, on the way," Luke responded.

He replaced the mic and glanced at his partner. "The passenger always handles the mic. That way the driver can keep his hands on the wheel and his eyes on the road."

A few minutes later, the radio crackled again. "Wagon 61, make that 16th Street and Bell Road for Six-eleven."

"10-4," Luke replied.

Officer Styles sat motionless. The color had drained from his face.

"Write that address down," Luke cautioned. "Don't rely on your memory. Something may distract us on the way and it's easy to forget where you're supposed to be going if it isn't written down. If you get in the habit of doing that, it might save an officer from getting the shit stomped out of him or even killed. Sometimes a few seconds can make the difference between life and death."

Styles picked up the notepad and with shaky hands, slipped a pen from the pocket of his shirt while glancing hesitantly at his partner.

"What was that address again?" he asked.

"Forget the initial address. The officer said he'd meet us at 16th Street and Bell." Luke was starting to lose patience. "You're really going to have to pay attention to the radio and write things down as soon as they come out. Are you OK? You look pale."

"Yeah," was the rookie's only reply.

"Where the hell were you guys? In South Phoenix?" Joe Biller groused when the wagon pulled up.

Luke smiled. He sympathized with the officer. It always seemed to take forever when waiting for a backup or an ambulance.

"We had to stop for coffee and donuts first since we had to drive half-way to Flagstaff just to pick up a docile drunk," Luke teased.

"Yeah, well. This docile drunk is over six feet tall and weighs nearly 300 pounds. He damned near kicked my ass. He's had a few drinks, but I didn't arrest him for that. He's under arrest for assault. He beat the shit out of his old lady. It took two of us to get him in the car. But Six-twelve had to leave on another call. I was hoping this asshole wouldn't kick the windows out before you got here."

Luke looked in the back seat of the police car at the glaring prisoner. "He doesn't look so tough," he chided. "My partner can probably handle him alone."

Biller glanced at the rookie who was still standing by the open door of the wagon.

"Isn't that right, Styles?" Luke teased.

Officer Styles face was white as chalk as he slowly walked towards the two officers. "Since he's already cuffed and settled down, maybe it would be better just to take him to jail in the police car instead of trying to put him in the wagon," he said.

"Open the back door of the wagon or I'm dumping him out and you two can deal with him," Biller spat.

Luke opened the wagon's double doors before approaching

the police car and its surly prisoner. He braced himself and swung the car door open.

"Step out slowly," Luke ordered.

The prisoner did as directed, and with Luke and Biller on each arm, walked slowly to the wagon and crawled in without a struggle. Once safely inside, the prisoner was ordered to face away from the door and kneel. Luke removed the handcuffs and handed them back to Officer Biller.

"Have a seat," he said.

The prisoner did as directed and settled into a corner near the cab.

"That went well," Luke said. "Guess he was tired out from beating his wife and fighting you guys."

"It wasn't his wife he beat up," Biller corrected. "It was his mother."

"What the hell? That big pile of shit beat up his mother?" It was difficult for Luke to believe that anyone would hit his mother, especially someone as big as the prisoner. He glanced around for his wagon partner, but Styles was already inside the cab.

"Some partner you got there," Biller said. "Where the hell was he when we transferred the prisoner? I wasn't paying that much attention, but I don't recall seeing him anywhere near."

Luke didn't comment. He'd noticed the same thing.

The ride downtown was made in silence. Luke considered asking about his partner's lack of participation, but decided to wait until they got to the *chute*, a narrow entry-way to the back door of the police station. He would see how Styles handled the situation when they had to escort the prisoner into the station and up the jail elevator.

Luke threw open the back door of the paddy wagon. "Come on out of there," he ordered. If the prisoner was going to fight, Luke was ready for him. Any man who beat up his mother didn't deserve to be handled with kid gloves.

The prisoner did as directed and offered no resistance as the officers grasped him by the arms and escorted him into the station.

The elevator ride to the jail on the top floor of the building was always an adventure when escorting an unruly prisoner. Officers were often bruised and battered by the time they reached the booking area.

Styles had squeezed himself into a corner instead of holding onto the prisoner as his senior partner was doing. His face was still a pasty white. The prisoner kept staring at the rookie officer and shaking his head. But the ride was quiet and uneventful. The booking procedure went equally as well.

On the ride back to the squad area, Luke glanced at his junior partner. Was Styles afraid to get into a fight? If not, why did he act so strangely with the prisoner?

Color had returned to Styles' face and he seemed more at ease. Maybe it was all Luke's imagination. For some strange reason, Luke didn't believe his partner was a coward. There must be a good excuse for the way he acted.

"What was the deal when we picked up the prisoner from Six-eleven? You acted like you were scared. If that scared you, then you're in the wrong line of work." Luke hadn't planned to be so direct, but the words came out.

His partner barely glanced at him before turning his head away. "I don't know what you're talking about. You each had a hold of the guy's arms. What was I supposed to do, hang onto his legs?"

Styles had a point. There wasn't much he could have done except to stand by in case there was trouble.

"Maybe you're right," Luke conceded. "Maybe you're right."

CHAPTER TEN

Emily gazed through the living room window onto Larkspur Drive for several minutes before returning to the kitchen to check the time. Luke was at work and Rebecca and Michael were at summer camp with their church group. She had enrolled Amy in a half-day pre-school program that ran six weeks during the summer. The child should have been home by now.

A few more glances through the front window proved fruitless. Emily walked out to the carport and down the driveway to the sidewalk. She could see the school at the end of the block, but Amy was nowhere in sight. If a student had to stay after for some reason, surely the parents would have been notified. She started to panic. What if something happened? Maybe Amy got lost on her way home. Maybe she got run over and was lying somewhere injured and alone.

Emily rushed into the house and grabbed a bottle from the medicine cabinet. "Stop it," she said aloud, disgusted with herself for succumbing to such unrealistic fears. She slammed the bottle down without opening it. "She's probably still at school playing on the swings."

Amy had been late before when she wandered onto the playground prior to coming home, but this time it felt different.

Emily snapped a leash on Skippy and headed out the door. She would walk the dog and check on Amy at the same time.

The school playground was deserted when Emily arrived. She went to the principal's office and tied Skippy to the outer door knob before going inside.

The secretary was seated at her desk with a phone to her ear, obviously discussing one of the students with an irate parent.

"I'm sorry you feel that way, Mrs. Blotz," the secretary said as she seemed more absorbed with the official looking documents she was working on than with the telephone conversation. "We do everything we can to ensure each child's emotional welfare as well as their academic one, and we cannot permit foul language to be used at school."

Emily couldn't help but respect the restraint exercised by the secretary. She certainly had excellent telephone manners. And all the while she was talking on the phone trying to pacify an angry parent, she was working on papers. Remarkable!

Emily stood quietly as the secretary continued with her conversation.

"No, I didn't hear it. But several students did, and it is not something that can be tolerated. We…Yes, I know you pay taxes. We all pay taxes. And all of us at this facility do our best to see that all students are protected and treated fairly. I…"

The secretary slowly placed the phone back in its cradle. "She hung up on me," she said to no one in particular.

The secretary seemed to notice Emily for the first time. "Hello," she said. "May I help you?"

"Yes," Emily said. "I'm Emily Canfield. My daughter, Amy, is in Miss Tillford's class. Amy isn't home yet. Is she still in class?"

The secretary slowly shook her head. "Her class was dismissed more than a half-hour ago. I'll check the room to see if she lingered for some reason."

Emily untied Skippy and followed the secretary to a classroom a few doors down from the office. They both glanced inside. The room was empty.

Emily's heart sank. "Where could she be?" she asked.

"Let's check the playground. Some of the kids…"

"I've already done that. She isn't there. No one is there."

Emily retorted.

She started to panic. She should have brought her pills. She should have taken one before she left. She should have…

Emily took a deep breath and exhaled slowly, just as Dr. Feldman suggested when he prescribed the medication. Another deep breath. 1…2…3…4…5…She counted slowly as the air gradually escaped from her lungs.

It didn't help. She started to hyperventilate. Her lungs ached. She clutched her chest. The aching pressure was getting worse. It was a heart attack for sure this time. No. Not now. Amy was in trouble. This was no time to give in to her emotions. She must stay strong. A few more deep breaths. The pain in her chest slowly subsided. Her breathing returned to normal.

"Mrs. Canfield, are you all right?" There was a concerned look on the secretary's face as she moved closer. "Would you like to come in and sit down for a bit? I'm sure your daughter is just fine. Let's go into the office. I'll call the parents of the other students in her class to see if she went home with one of them."

"I'm OK," Emily breathlessly replied. "You call the other parents. I'll go home and see if Amy is there. Maybe she went home through the alley. Call me at home after you call the parents."

"Yes. That's probably the best thing to do," the secretary

agreed. She hurried to the office as Emily led Skippy away. He, too, seemed in a hurry to get home.

Emily threw open the carport door and led Skippy inside.

"Amy, are you in here?" Her question went unanswered. "Amy? Amy?"

A quick check of the house proved fruitless. There was no sign of her daughter anywhere.

Emily unhooked Skippy's leash and hung it on its hook near the front door. She returned to the kitchen and glanced at the clock above the sink. The hands were spinning wildly. Time was passing too fast for the hands to catch up. What was happening? Was she finally going completely mad? Her head was about to explode. The room was growing dark. She grabbed the counter to steady herself, but her arms were too weak. Her legs began to buckle. No. She couldn't let herself succumb to the darkness. She couldn't give in. She needed every bit of emotional as well as physical strength. Amy was in trouble. Luke. She needed to call Luke. He would know what to do. He would find their daughter.

Emily summoned all of her strength and staggered to the wall phone near the kitchen door. "Thank God," she breathed when a voice answered. She didn't even get the name. She didn't care who it was. "Hello," she said. "This is Emily Canfield. My husband is Officer Luke Canfield. Could you get hold of him and tell him to call home right away?"

"Is it an emergency?" the voice asked.

"I wouldn't have called if it wasn't," Emily angrily replied.

"I'll give him the message," the voice said. "Do you need help right away? Should I send an officer?"

Emily hesitated. "Just tell Luke to call me."

***

The day had started out relatively uneventful for Wagon 61. They pushed a stalled motorist from the middle lane of Camelback Road and hauled an abandoned bicycle to the impound lot.

It was nearing 11 a.m. when they received a family fight call to an upscale residence off Central Avenue. The beat car was assigned the call. The wagon officers would make his backup.

When he first became an officer, it had surprised Luke to get calls of family fights among the more affluent. He soon discovered that status and wealth doesn't make people immune from physical conflict in a relationship.

Luke recognized the address as soon as it came out. It belonged to a city fireman who was known to dislike cops. He was considered armed and dangerous, but somehow, he always managed to talk his way out of being arrested.

It was suspected that the fireman had a friend in the upper echelon of the police department who was looking out for him. It also didn't hurt that his father was a member of the city council.

Luke filled his partner in on the situation. "We may have to shoot this asshole, so be ready. I heard he got the drop on an officer the last time the police were called, but for some reason they didn't book him. I don't intend to let that happen with us."

Officer Styles remained silent as they made their way to the address and pulled up on a side street adjacent to the sprawling residence. They noticed a police car parked in front, but the officer was nowhere in sight.

"I'm going to slip around the side of the house and see if I can hear or see anything. You stay by the wagon in case I need you to relay something on the radio," Luke directed.

Luke glanced back as he headed for the corner of the house. Officer Styles had followed his training officer's orders and stood at the open door of the wagon with the mic in hand.

"Hey, Luke!" Styles yelled as he put down the mic. "Radio says to call your house. Your wife called and said you should call home right away."

"What the hell now?" Luke grumbled. "Well, she wouldn't

have called if it wasn't important." He started back to the wagon, but suddenly got the urge to check the exterior of the house to see if anything needed his immediate attention.

As he rounded the corner of the house, he came upon the suspect. The man's back was to Luke. A shotgun held tightly in his hands was trained on the beat officer assigned to the call.

Luke slowly slid his weapon out of its holster and leveled it at the back of the suspect's head. He wasn't quite sure what to do. He couldn't just shoot the guy in the back without warning. Besides, if he fired, it may cause a reflex action. The shotgun could go off, killing the officer being held at gunpoint.

Maybe he could sneak up on the man, distract him and grab the gun, or maybe hit him in the head with his revolver.

Luke crept slowly forward, his gun raised to strike the back of the man's head. His other hand poised to grab the shotgun. He was still undecided as to his exact course of action, but it would come to him when the time came. It always had. Strange how calm he felt. It seemed the more stressful the situation, the calmer he became. It was as if another entity had taken over. One with a fatalistic outlook. It was out of Luke's hands. Whatever was going to happen would happen. That is the way it is supposed to be. That is the way it is already written in "The Book."

Before Luke could get close enough to carry out his plan,

the suspect spun around. The muzzle of the shotgun was now less than ten feet away from Luke's belly, and the crazed look on the man's face gave every indication that he was about to pull the trigger.

***

Shortly after Emily hung up the phone, it rang.

"Thank God! Luke?" she asked.

"Mrs. Canfield, this is Mavis Waters at the school. Has your daughter come home yet?"

Emily suddenly became very cold. The blackness again. She placed one hand on the wall beside the phone and shivered as she tried to maintain her balance.

"Hello? Mrs. Canfield? Are you there?" The secretary's voice bit through her haze.

"No," Emily gasped. "Amy isn't here."

"I called the parents of the other children in your daughter's class. There were several that I couldn't get hold of, but the ones I talked with haven't seen Amy."

Emily didn't respond. She tried, but her voice was gone. She swallowed several times and licked her lips.

The secretary's voice again cut through the fog. "I will keep trying to contact the parents I was unable to get hold of. I'm sure Amy must have gone home with one of the other kids. We will keep looking. If she shows up, please let me know."

The phone in Emily's hand became very heavy. She tried to hang it up, but she was unable to reach that high. Funny, it normally hung below her shoulders, but now she had to reach up. What was happening? Had she shrunk, or had everything suddenly gotten bigger?

The off-white walls turned gray. Maybe she was going blind. She reached for the wall. It was too far away. Everything was out of reach. Everything, that is, except the floor.

***

Time stood still. Luke had often heard it said that your life flashes before you just before you die. But nothing came to mind except how big the muzzle of the shotgun looked.

Neither man uttered a word. Each stood silently, staring at the other, seemingly frozen in time.

The summer sun was relentless in its intensity. Luke stood glued to the spot, his gun up near his shoulder in a thwarted attempt to strike the suspect in the head. Rivulets of sweat rolled down his forehead and into his eyes, causing a burning sensation.

Still, he didn't blink and he didn't move.

He managed to lift his gaze from the muzzle of the shotgun to the suspect's face. It was a tortured face; one that had reached the breaking point; the look of someone who had crossed the threshold of reason. There was no turning back.

Quietly and calmly, Luke said, "I'm not moving."

The suspect said nothing. He just continued to point the shotgun at Luke's belly, his finger on the trigger, his eyes unblinking and a grotesque expression on his face.

Seconds slipped by without movement from either man as the sun beat down mercilessly. Sweat continued to trickle down Luke's face. His eyes felt like they were on fire, and his raised arm felt like it was made of lead.

The six inch Colt Luke was holding seemed to weigh a ton. He couldn't hold it up any longer. He stared into the suspect's eyes. If the crazed man was going to pull the trigger, Luke was going to make the shooter look him in the eyes while he did it.

A thought suddenly came to him. What if I get killed while Emily is waiting for me to call? He was about to get killed and his only concern was that he had to call his wife. In another setting, it would have been laughably ironic. But it was too realistic, too probable, to be funny. Luke needed to get control of the situation and call his wife. He had never let her down before and he wasn't about to start now.

"I'm going to have to put my arm down," Luke calmly said. "I can't hold it up any longer, so you do whatever you think you have to do."

Slowly and deliberately, Luke began lowering his arm. The gunman's finger started to tighten on the trigger, but suddenly stopped. A look of surprise and indecision flooded his face. He hesitated for just an instant before backing away and slipping into the house.

Luke breathed a deep sigh of relief. The suspect had come to his senses just in time. From the look on his face, he must have even scared himself with his actions. Luke walked over to a shady part of the house and leaned against the wall. The other officer who had been held at gunpoint was nowhere in sight.

After a few minutes, Luke regained his composure. Backup officers had arrived and surrounded the house. Sergeant Hastings was among them.

Luke explained what had happened.

"Never let a suspect back in the house once you get them out," the sergeant said. "Where is the other officer who was being held at gunpoint?"

"I don't know. I never saw him again," Luke replied. "He's probably around the front, or maybe he's still cleaning out his pants."

"Well, we've got to get the guy out of the house. Did you try talking to him?"

"Hell no, Sarge. I haven't spoken with him since he went back inside. I was just trying not to get shot rather than trying to prevent him from going back in. In fact, I hoped he would."

Hastings gave Luke a disapproving look before heading to the front of the house.

Luke trailed behind.

When they reached the front door, Hastings yelled, "Come on out of there. We need to talk with you."

The only response was the metallic action of a shotgun. Luke stepped to the side, a good distance away from the door. He was surprised to find his sergeant standing directly in front.

Before he could comment on the dangers of standing in the line of fire, Hastings reared back and kicked the middle of the door. His foot broke through, trapping his shoe, but the lock held. The sergeant hopped around on one leg while trying unsuccessfully to pull his foot from the hollow core door.

The unmistakable sound of a shotgun shell entering the chamber caused Luke to react without thinking. He grabbed Sergeant Hastings around the waist and yanked with all his might. The two officers ended up sprawled on their backs several feet from the front door.

Luke looked back from where he'd landed. It was a bizarre sight. Hastings' shoe was still embedded in the door, but the sergeant had immediately jumped up and was hopping around on one foot trying to keep from getting his sock dirty.

The scene was something out of *Keystone Cops*. Regardless of the seriousness of the situation, Luke busted out laughing at the absurdity of it all. Everything seemed so ridiculous. *Life* seemed ridiculous.

Luke rose to his feet, calmly walked over, pulled his sergeant's shoe from the door and handed it to him. If the suspect hadn't pulled the trigger up to this point, chances were he wouldn't do it now.

Hastings grabbed the shoe and retreated to a safer location before sitting down and putting it on. Luke went with him.

The two officers were making their way back to the front door when Captain Joe Sands pulled up to the curb.

Hastings hurried to meet him. Luke tagged along. He was curious to hear how his sergeant was going to explain the situation.

Captain Sands was a veteran of nearly thirty years on the job. He had a reputation of being a good officer, but after being shot in the gut during a family fight call he had become a little gun shy. The fact that he was a Captain kept him behind a desk most of the time. But today he was duty-officer. That meant he was expected to physically respond to serious crime scenes.

Sands wasn't nearly as tall as Canfield or Hastings, but he was a lot heavier. He stood silently as the sergeant hurriedly explained the situation.

"He hasn't fired any shots, but we heard him racking a shotgun so we consider him armed and dangerous," Hastings said.

"He held one officer at gunpoint, and when I walked up he held a shotgun on me. I thought he was going to shoot, but he must have suddenly come to his senses and stepped back into the house," Luke interjected.

Captain Sands didn't respond. He barely glanced at the officers before making his way up the walkway to the front door.

"Carl," he yelled as he knocked on the front door. "This is Joe Sands. What the hell are you doing in there? Open this damned door and let me in. I'm coming in alone. Open the door."

After a few minutes, Luke heard the click of a lock.

Sands motioned to a location out of sight of the front door. "You two wait over there," he said.

"This guy is dangerous, Captain," Luke hurriedly replied. "He held a shotgun on another officer and me. We should probably go in with you."

"I'm going in alone. Do as you're told." The steely tone and disapproving look from Sands caused Sergeant Hastings to immediately move to the designated location. Luke reluctantly followed. He watched apprehensively as the door swung open and the Captain disappeared inside.

It was difficult for Luke to understand why Captain Sands would take such a chance with an obviously emotionally disturbed man. He was either very brave or exceptionally foolhardy.

Luke turned to his sergeant. "What in the hell could the Captain be thinking, going into a house with a guy that's already threatened two officers and is obviously nuts?" he asked.

"I don't know. We'll just have to trust his judgment. We need to stay close in case he needs us," Hastings replied.

"I need to call home," Luke said. "Radio said my wife asked that I call right away."

"If it was serious enough she would have asked to see an officer," Hastings said. "I don't know about you guys with your wives calling all the time. It would have to be something pretty serious before my wife called me at work."

Luke bit his lip to keep from exploding. He knew once he let his anger get the better of him, he'd either be in jail or looking for another job. He moved away from his sergeant.

"I'd better check on my partner. I'll be right back." He

headed to the wagon.

Gary Styles was still standing by the open door with a firm grip on the mic. At least the rookie could follow directions.

It took a few minutes for Luke to calm down before he could explain to his partner what was going on. "The guy is holed up in the house with a shotgun. The Captain is in there with him. Apparently, he doesn't think the guy is that much of a threat. But the son of a bitch pointed a shotgun at me and another officer, so as far as I'm concerned he's bought and paid for."

Officer Styles remained silent as Luke continued. "Guess it isn't necessary to stand by here. We'd better go to the front door and be ready to grab the guy when the Captain brings him out. We got at least two counts of *assault with a deadly weapon* on him. I can't wait to book this asshole." Luke headed to the front of the house, his partner trailing.

They joined Sergeant Hastings at the spot originally designated by the Captain. The desert sun threw off heat like a blast furnace, soaking the officers with sweat as they scrambled for shade next to some oleanders.

Luke was careful not to touch the plant. The stalks grew outrageously tall and the flowers were beautiful, but he'd heard that the leaves and stems were poisonous. Many Phoenix streets, however, were lined with oleanders and people continued to plant them in their yards. He often wondered about that. But right now, all that mattered was the fact that they provided shade. It was a welcome relief from the blazing sun.

After hearing nothing from inside the house, Luke again turned to his sergeant. "I need to get the hell out of here so I can call my wife. There's some kind of emergency or she wouldn't have called."

"That was at least a half-hour ago," Hastings replied. "If there *was* an emergency, you're way too late to do anything about it now. If you'd like, I'll call radio and tell them to have an officer stop by your house to check on things, but it wouldn't make much sense if you left now."

"You're probably right," Luke reluctantly agreed.

***

"Mrs. Canfield. Mrs. Canfield. Emily." The voice sounded distant, but it slowly cut through the fog in Emily's brain. She opened her eyes and stared across the linoleum covered floor. It felt cool on her face. She closed her eyes and started to give in to the darkness once again.

"Emily, wake up," the voice repeated. A hand on her shoulder shook her gently.

Emily opened her eyes and was startled to see a stranger kneeling beside her. Instinctively, she tried to scramble away.

"It's OK," the voice said. "Don't be alarmed. I'm Dennis Creech, a police officer. We've met before."

Emily was suddenly wide awake. "Where...? How...?"

Creech rose to his feet and took her by the arm. "I brought your daughter home. She's fine. Nothing to worry about. Can you sit up?"

"Where is she?" Emily asked. She glanced quickly around and staggered to her feet.

"Take it easy. She's fine. I told her to wait in the car and surprise you. I didn't think it would be a good idea for her to see you lying on the floor. You wait here and I'll bring her in. Are you OK now?"

"Yes, yes. I'm OK. Bring her in please," Emily pleaded.

Emily was at the front door to greet her when Amy walked in with a big grin. "Hi Mommy. Did I surprise you?"

"Are you OK? Are you hurt?" Emily asked. She gave her daughter a hug before holding her at arm's length and giving her the once-over. "Where were you? I was worried sick. Why didn't you come right home after school? Where were you?" she repeated.

"I can fill you in on the details," Creech softly said.

"Maybe Amy could get washed up or watch cartoons while we talk." A glare from Emily prompted him to add, "If that's all right with you."

Emily nodded. "Go get washed up and I'll fix you a snack." She gave Amy another hug before sending her down the hall to the bathroom.

As soon as Amy was out of earshot, Creech began his explanation. "I was in the area when I saw a little girl walking in the alley a few blocks south. It appeared she was following a dog. She told me who she was and I brought her home. Nothing much more to it."

For the first time since she had awakened on the floor, Emily took a good look at the plain clothes officer with his infectious smile and slicked-back hair. "Thank you," she said. "I don't know how you happened along when you did, but I'm very grateful. I can't thank you enough. The least I can do is call your boss and tell him about your good police work."

Creech smiled slightly as he shook his head. "I would rather you didn't. I'm supposed to be following up on another case across town. My sergeant would probably get a little upset if he found I was somewhere else. In fact, I'd appreciate it if you didn't even mention it to Luke. He'd probably think there was something going on between us."

"Well, OK, I won't say anything," Emily said. "But I won't forget what you did today. If something happened to one of the kids I don't think I could take it."

As Creech turned to go, Emily put her hand on his arm. "How about a bite to eat before you go? That's the least I can do. I'm going to fix a snack for Amy. I can fix you one too."

"Thanks, but I'd better be going," Creech said as he headed for the door. "Aside from the circumstance, it was good to see you again."

Emily stood silently for several minutes after the detective left. Luke was right; there was something strange about him. He was as handsome a man as she'd ever seen. He was also an excellent conversationalist with impeccable manners, and yet there didn't appear to be any women in his life. And his explanation that he was in the area and just happened to see Amy in the alley didn't make any sense either. Especially since he was supposed to be on the other side of town. And how did he know enough to come in and find Emily on the floor? There was something mysterious and yet comforting about the man. Even though she hardly knew him, she felt relaxed and safe in his presence.

"Where's my snack?" Amy's question snapped her out of her rumination.

"Coming up." Emily smiled as she pulled the jelly and

peanut butter from the cupboard.

***

Nearly half an hour had passed before Captain Sands came out of the house alone.

"You two can return to your vehicle and stand by to wagon a prisoner," the Captain said as he nodded toward the two patrol officers. "Sergeant, I need to talk with you."

"Finally," Luke muttered as he and his partner made their way to the wagon. "I don't know what took so long for the Captain to realize this guy needs to go to jail."

After a few minutes, Sergeant Hastings joined them. "The Captain decided to book the wife instead of the man," he said. "She always starts the fight and he's the one who suffers. He's a city fireman. If we book him he'll probably be fired. We can resolve the problem by booking her, since she's the one who caused it."

"What?" Luke exclaimed. "Are you shitting me? That son of a bitch belongs in jail. And he should be fired. Maybe I should talk to the Captain. He probably didn't understand that the guy held me and another officer at gunpoint."

"He knows all that," Hastings said. "We're to book the

wife."

Luke slowly shook his head as he climbed into the driver's side of the wagon. "Get in," he ordered his partner. "Sorry, Sarge. We have more pressing things to do than wagon a woman who is falsely arrested just to save a criminal from being fired." He didn't wait for a response. He slammed the gear shift into drive and headed for Brookshire's.

Hastings never made a move to stop him, he just turned to the beat officer who had poked his head around the corner of the house to see what all the commotion was about. There was no doubt in Luke's mind that Hastings would order the beat officer to take the woman to jail.

It was hard for Luke to believe that a police Captain would cave in to a guy who held two officers at gunpoint just because he happened to work for the same city. It didn't make any sense.

Luke needed a cup of coffee. He also needed to call his wife. Maybe she'd had another panic attack.

The restaurant had its usual lunchtime crowd. The two officers were met at the counter and escorted to an empty booth in back. Luke could feel other patron's eyes follow their every move as they made their way through the maze of tables and booths.

It was nothing new. People always stared at uniformed

cops. It used to make Luke feel self-conscious, but he had gotten used to it. Anyone that close to you with the power to put you in jail or even take your life was bound to cause some attention. He suspected the interest was more out of curiosity than anything else.

He walked over to the pay phone near the restrooms and dialed the city operator. After giving the operator the phone number, and hearing his number dialed and the clink of a coin, he fished his dime out of the coin return.

"Hello," Emily answered. Her voice was weak.

"Hi. What's going on?" Luke asked.

"Nothing now," Emily replied.

"You wanted me to call? What's the emergency?" Luke couldn't help but sound a little disgusted. After all, he had nearly gotten killed by a shotgun wielding maniac, and his wife wanted him to call home for nothing? What the hell was she thinking?

"Everything is taken care of. I got worried because I couldn't find Amy. Instead of coming straight home from school, she followed some stray dog around the neighborhood. But she's here now safe and sound and everything is fine."

"OK...well...I'll talk to you later." Luke hung up the phone and stood silently for a few minutes. Emily was leaving something out. He could tell it in her voice. But it was probably a draw. He'd be leaving something out as well. There was no way he was going to tell her he had almost gotten killed by a maniac with a shotgun. "No way," he muttered as he made his way to the booth where his partner waited.

Little was said during lunch. Luke ordered a bowl of vegetable soup and a cup of coffee. He was too disgusted with the Captain's decision not to book the fireman to eat much of anything. But no matter his mood, he could always eat a bowl of soup.

Officer Styles settled for a salad and a glass of iced tea. Luke had to admit it made more sense than hot soup and coffee. But soup was a staple on the farm, even in the summer, and it always made him feel better emotionally when he had a belly full of food like his mother used to make.

As Luke drained his third cup of coffee, a man approached. Luke saw him coming, and even though they'd never met, he felt as if he already knew him. This was from hearing other officer's tales of their encounters with Jimmy Granger.

"Hello boys." Granger grinned as he pulled up a chair from a nearby table. "Mind if I join you?"

For some reason, Luke harbored no animosity toward the safe burglar. He probably should. After all, the man was a known criminal. He stole other people's hard earned money.

Luke knew all of that, yet he felt empathy for the man. He sensed Jimmy Granger was a tortured soul. It was as if a thousand voices were screaming for help, trying to break free of their imprisonment in his mind.

"Why don't you pull up a chair and join us?" Luke chuckled. "How are you Jimmy? Staying out of trouble?"

"Have we met before?" Granger cautiously asked.

Luke shook his head. "No," he said. "But I've heard so much about you, it's as if I already know you."

The comment seemed to unnerve the safe burglar.

"I really didn't intend to interrupt your lunch," Granger said. "Don't believe everything you hear about me. I'm really not a bad guy, and I'm never armed, so don't shoot me if you ever happen to catch me in a compromising situation. I would never resist, so don't shoot me."

"If you're afraid of being shot, I suggest you switch occupations. Some cops, kinda like my partner here," Luke nodded to Officer Styles, "shoots first and asks questions later."

Styles looked bewildered as he glanced back and forth between his training officer and the known burglar.

"Well, I won't bother you further," Granger replied. "I just wanted to say that I admire the work you do and I would like to buy you both lunch."

"Thanks for the offer, but we couldn't accept," Luke said. "I'm sure you understand."

Granger sat quietly for a minute, then nodded. "Yes, I quite understand," he said before pushing back his chair.

He rose to his feet and stared at Luke. "As soon as I walked up, I felt like you knew everything about me. Yet I felt nothing judgmental. That's the first time I have ever spoken to a cop that I didn't feel like they wanted to shoot me down where I stood. How can you know so much about the inner me when I hardly know myself?"

A thin smile broke the plain of Luke's mouth. "Life is like a painting," he said. "Sometimes the image becomes clearer from a distance. But I've learned a long time ago not to judge the flaws I perceive in others, because they're usually a reflection of my own."

Granger shook his head. "Too bad I didn't run into you when I was younger," he said. "Before I got off on the wrong foot. Things might have been different."

With a heavy sigh, Granger replaced the chair that he'd pulled over from a nearby table. He slowly made his way to the register and paid his bill before leaving the restaurant.

Luke watched him go, knowing that Granger was just one of many who from early childhood, seemed destined for a life they were unable to control. Circumstance and situation drove them in a pre-programmed direction they were powerless to prevent.

Maybe the reason Luke could relate was because it had happened to him. At the age of nine, his destiny was determined. He'd tried to fight it. But some unknown force always won out. He was the puppet, and someone else was pulling the strings.

***

Emily uncovered the scalloped potatoes and ham, and turned the oven up a notch. Luke would soon be home and he liked his casseroles browned. If he had his way, everything would be cooked until there wasn't a drop of moisture left. She was often embarrassed when they ate out. He always told the waiter to cook his meat well enough so he could break it instead of cut it. Emily liked her meat rare. She shook her head. Just one more thing to show how little they had in common.

She had simmered down considerably since she'd taken her meds. She was still angry that Luke hadn't called sooner. More than an hour had gone by before he'd called. *Guess that goes to show how important we are. Or maybe it's just me. If one of the kids had called, he would have responded sooner.* She shook her head, disgusted with herself for thinking that way. Still…

I bet he would have dropped everything and called if he

knew Dennis Creech was here. I can't wait to see his face when I tell him. The thought resulted in a thin smile and a soft chuckle. It was quickly wiped away by another thought. *No, he'll just turn it against me and question my relationship with Dennis rather than admit his neglect in failing to call me sooner.*

The sound of Luke's truck pulling into the driveway caused Emily to take a deep breath and concentrate on last-minute supper preparations. She pulled the casserole from the oven and made sure the coffee pot was full.

Rebecca had already set the table before retreating to her room, so that much was done. Michael and Amy were also in their rooms doing who knows what. At least they weren't underfoot. Their small kitchen couldn't accommodate three kids milling about with the pretense of helping when there was cooking to be done.

"Hi," Luke said as he strolled in. "Is everybody still in one piece around here?"

He grasped Emily by the shoulders and gave her a peck on the forehead before grabbing a cup of coffee and sitting down at his usual place at the table.

Emily didn't respond right away. She'd been angry. But suddenly she wasn't. She didn't know how she felt. The presence of Dennis Creech seemed to instill a quiet confidence in her that was difficult to explain.

She glanced at Luke who was sipping his coffee while eyeing her with that same stupid grin he'd often displayed when he thought she was being overly dramatic about something.

"Everyone is fine," Emily replied. "I got worried when Amy didn't come home from school on time. I went to the school to get her, but she wasn't there. No one knew where she was. I called the briefing station and told whoever answered the phone to have you call home right away. How come you didn't call sooner? I was really worried."

"I'm sorry about that," Luke replied. "I was on a family fight call that took longer than expected and I couldn't get to a phone. In a situation like that, just call the emergency number and they'll send an officer out. I can't always get to a phone right away."

"That's probably what I should have done," Emily said. "But at the time, I guess I wasn't thinking clearly. Anyway, she's home safe and sound. She'd followed a stray dog around the neighborhood."

Luke rose from the table and went to Amy's room. She was busy changing clothes on one of her many dolls as he walked in. He gathered her up in his arms and gave her a kiss on the cheek. "I hear you've had a busy day," he said. "Your mommy was worried about you. We love you and we get scared when we don't know where you are. Promise me you'll come straight home from school from now on. Otherwise, I'll worry too."

"I promise," Amy replied. She wriggled free from Luke's arms and continued to dress her doll.

Luke returned to the kitchen and resumed his seat at the table. He quietly sipped his coffee while Emily put the finishing touches on the evening meal.

Emily suppressed a grin after overhearing the conversation between Luke and Amy. She was pleasantly surprised that Amy hadn't mentioned being brought home by a police officer. Dennis Creech's timely visit would remain her secret. It felt good to know something Luke didn't know. It was a harmless something, but it felt good none-the-less. It gave her a feeling of empowerment.

CHAPTER ELEVEN

Late one Sunday morning, Wagon 61 received a family fight call to a residence near 16th Street and Bell Road. A woman had frantically called and said she was having family troubles. The address sounded vaguely familiar. Luke shook his head in disgust. Another family fight.

It hadn't been that long ago since his encounter with the shotgun-wielding fireman. The Captain's refusal to book the son of a bitch still irritated Luke. "What in the hell is the matter with people? Why the hell do they continue to live together if they can't get along?" His rhetorical questions went unanswered.

It was another scorcher. The blacktop shimmered with heat, casting slivers of light that flashed ahead as they made their way up Cave Creek Road.

Luke glanced at his partner. Gary Styles' face was white as a ghost. His hand shook when he replaced the mic. He jotted down the address that he kept staring at as though trying to visualize what was going on there.

They were less than a mile away when the call came out. Within a few minutes they pulled up to the residence, a small white house mid-block. The front door was standing open.

Even before coming to a stop, a body could be seen lying on the walkway outside the front door. It was that of a huge man, face down, his arms outstretched. A pool of blood around his head was rapidly drying in the searing heat of the relentless sun.

"No, no, no," Styles cried as he hurried past the body.

"Hey, wait up, Gary. Don't go in there!" Luke yelled

Styles paid him no mind. He bolted through the open door with Luke trying to catch up.

After pulling his gun, Luke cautiously approached the doorway and quickly scanned the room before stepping inside. Styles was already out of sight.

With gun at the ready, Luke quickly searched the house, wondering what the hell had gotten into his partner. Styles appeared to be afraid of his own shadow. Now, he rushes into a house where a murderer might be holed up and he didn't even draw his gun?

Luke entered a back bedroom to find his partner weeping uncontrollably while kneeling beside the lifeless body of a small woman.

The thought that Styles had finally cracked under stress crossed Luke's mind as he gingerly asked, "What's going on? Do you know this woman?"

"My mother," Styles sobbed. "My mother."

An icy hand grabbed Luke by the heart. His partner's mother dead? Why the hell didn't Styles say something about it being his mother's address when the call came out?

Luke holstered his weapon after seeing a small handgun near the woman's body. The only sign of trauma was some blood on her hair.

Dead bodies all had that same emptiness about them. They reminded Luke of an animal after taxidermy. The physical characteristics were still there, but the spirit had gone, leaving behind a silhouette of the former self; a lifeless hulk of skin ready for stuffing.

Regardless of the fact that the body was his partner's mother, it was still a crime scene and must be handled as one.

"I'm sorry about your mother, but you're going to have to get up and back away. Let's go in the other room. This is a crime scene," Luke said softly.

Styles remained on his knees by the body.

"Get up. Let's get out of here," Luke said more forcefully.

He helped Styles to his feet and guided him into the kitchen.

"Sit here." Luke pulled a chair out from the table. "I'm going to check on the man outside. Do you know who it is?"

"My brother," Styles whispered.

"Your brother? The man outside is your brother? Are you sure?"

"My mother finally killed him. I knew it was going to happen. I should have done something. It's my fault. I should have done something."

It was difficult for Luke to accept what he was hearing. He couldn't even imagine such a thing. But it looked every bit like a murder/suicide.

He checked for vitals on the man face down on the walkway. Several small holes in his shirt appeared to have been made by bullets. One or more slugs had apparently caught him in the back of the head. He was obviously dead.

Luke went to the wagon and asked radio to notify the detective bureau and send an ambulance. He needed a qualified person to pronounce the bodies deceased. He grabbed some report forms and hurried back to the house where he joined his partner at the kitchen table.

Styles had quit sobbing and sat quietly, staring off into space.

"Do you want to tell me what was going on here?" Luke asked.

Styles remained silent for several minutes before turning to his partner.

"Do you remember when my brother–my half-brother actually–was arrested for beating up my mother?"

Luke shook his head.

"We wagoned him for Six-eleven. You didn't think I helped enough. Do you remember that? You ought to. You thought I was a coward. I was just scared this would happen. That's the only thing I was scared of. I guess he knocked her around for the last time."

It all came back. At the time, Luke couldn't imagine anyone beating up his mother, especially someone the size of the man lying outside the front door. But now, after seeing how tiny she was, it was even more incredulous. How could a big lout like that have hit his mother? It was beyond comprehension.

"I never said you were a coward. I just wondered why you seemed so timid about transporting the prisoner," Luke said defensively. "I know it doesn't help much to say, I'm sorry for your loss, but I truly am. I can't even imagine how I would feel if..."

It's all my fault.

Those words had echoed through Luke's brain time and time again since the age of nine. Just when he thought he could finally let go of the past, a word or two triggered the memory and started the blame process all over again. It was his fault that his little sister nearly drowned. It was his fault that she died at an early age. If only he had taken time to latch the gate. If only...

Styles was staring at Luke with a concerned look. He seemed to have forgotten his mother was lying dead in the back room.

"Sorry," Luke softly said. "Sometimes I have flashbacks of a time in my life that was not so great. I guess we all feel guilty about something. If not, we probably should. But why the hell didn't you tell me at the time that it was your brother we had in custody?"

"I didn't want to get fired," Styles said. "I was afraid if the department knew of my family troubles, they would figure I was a problem too. I didn't want to get fired," he repeated.

"You wouldn't have been held responsible for something your family members did," Luke said.

Styles failed to respond. He sobbed quietly as he brushed away tears. Luke was grateful when the awkward period was broken by the sound of a dying siren. An ambulance attendant rushed through the door.

"My partner is with the man on the ground," the attendant said. "Where's the other one?"

"In the back bedroom." Luke rose from his chair and led the way.

After a short examination, both mother and son were declared officially dead and the ambulance attendants hurried off to another call. The officers would have to remain at the scene until the detectives showed up.

Luke would like to have gotten his partner out of the house. But it was hotter than hell outside, and no telling how long they would have to wait for a detective. Hurry up and wait. Just like the Army.

Luke used the kitchen wall-phone to dial the Records Bureau and obtain a departmental report number. Detectives always liked for the initial officers to do as much preliminary work as they could without destroying evidence. Ordinarily, Luke wouldn't have touched anything, even the phone, in case it needed to be dusted for prints. But this was an obvious murder/suicide, and both victim and suspect were dead.

Luke had jotted down the ambulance attendants names, their arrival and departure times, and the time each person was pronounced dead. He had considered diverting his partner's pain by having him write the report, but Styles appeared in no shape to do anything except sit quietly.

After a short wait, a detective sauntered through the door. Dennis Creech. What were the chances? Luke shook his head.

"Hey, Rook. So you finally shot someone before they shot you," Creech chuckled. "But if you're going to do that, it's usually a good idea to shoot them in the front instead of the back. It always looks better."

"Hi, Dennis," Luke said. "I didn't know you were working homicide."

"I'm not," Creech smirked. "I just happened to be in the area. The dead body guys will be along shortly. I guess they just wanted me to make sure you didn't screw up the scene before they got here."

Luke felt the urge to verbally lash out, but he managed to hold it in check as he nodded toward Gary Styles sitting quietly at the table. "The one outside is my partner's brother. His mother is in the bedroom." He wanted to shut the detective up before he said anything more hurtful or embarrassing. Styles had been hurt enough.

"Did he shoot 'em?" Creech asked.

"Neither one of us shot anyone," Luke tersely replied. "It

appears she shot him and then shot herself." He led the detective to the bedroom.

Creech looked the woman over. "Looks like she put the barrel in her mouth and pulled the trigger. Women never like to mess up their face. They normally shoot themselves in the heart or through their open mouth. *Vanity of vanities; all is vanity,*" he quipped.

Luke was familiar with that Biblical quote, but he was surprised Dennis Creech had ever heard of it...or even heard of the Bible for that matter. He didn't seem the type.

After leaving a completed supplement report, the wagon officers returned to their vehicle. Creech would stay with the bodies until the homicide team arrived.

Luke picked up the mic and asked radio to have Sergeant Hastings meet them at the station. Gary Styles was in no shape to continue working. He wondered how his partner would ever come to terms with the scene he'd just witnessed. The trauma would last a lifetime. Of that, Luke was sure. He was a prime example. He wondered, however, why Dennis Creech always happened to be in the area whenever Luke was involved in anything serious. It was a ridiculous thought. Creech was like a bad cold: so aggravating that it seemed to come around more often than it actually did.

***

It had been nearly a year since Gary Styles quit the department and joined his father's accounting firm. The job appeared to be a much better fit than police work. Luke was back on nights, riding a beat. Instead of his usual assignment on the outer fringe of the city, however, he was now riding beat Six-twenty-one, a smaller, more centralized area. But also much busier.

He had gotten better at filling in his worksheet. He still lagged in writing tickets, but he had logged enough criminal and drunk driving arrests to keep Sergeant Hastings off his back.

It was nearing midnight when Luke got the call of a theft at a house in a more affluent area of his beat. Minor thefts were usually reported in the daytime, or at least a lot earlier in the evening. The nighttime hours were reserved for more serious crimes; unless, of course you were one of the elite.

Maybe the homeowner suddenly realized his garden hose was missing. That facetious thought and several others ran through Luke's mind as he made his way to the call.

The house was as pretentious as the address. Accent lights dotted the landscape, bathing the palm trees in colors of red, white, and blue. A walkway ran from the three car garage to the covered entry flanked by colorful beds of flowers. A dim light glowed through the lace curtains of a large picture window.

Luke rung the bell and waited. No one answered. He pushed the button again. Still no answer.

He was about to move away when the door slowly opened and a sultry voice whispered, "Hello officer. Please come in."

Luke's first impulse was to leave. Get the hell out of there as fast as his legs would carry him.

"How are you this fine evening?" the woman in the doorway asked.

"I'm fine," Luke answered. "You wanted to report a theft?"

"Come in. I won't bite," she teased.

Luke caught a whiff of gin as he brushed past her into the house.

"Have a seat on the couch and kick off your shoes. Can I get you a drink?"

He quickly scanned the room. A couch was the last place he wanted to sit. He wanted to keep as much distance as possible from the obviously drunk woman. But it was the only area with light enough to write his report.

"I'll take a cup of coffee if you have some." Luke really didn't want anything except to get out of there as quickly as possible. But he decided making coffee would keep the woman busy while he obtained the necessary information for his report. He didn't want to spend a minute more with the inebriated woman than he had to.

"I'm Beth." She edged closer. "What's your name?"

"I'm Officer Canfield."

"No, I mean what's your first name?"

Luke wanted to keep everything on a professional basis so she wouldn't confuse his visit with a social call, but he didn't want to make a big deal out of it. Some people wanted the officer's full name.

"Luke. My first name is Luke."

Beth was a woman whose demeanor clashed with the elegant furnishings. She fit closer to the mold of a low income, middle-aged, neglected and overweight housewife who had too much time on her hands. An open housecoat revealed a flimsy pale-yellow nightgown.

"What did you want to report stolen?" Luke asked. He continued to stand.

"I'll be with you in a minute. Have a seat." Beth headed to the kitchen.

Luke reluctantly eased down at the end of the couch and pulled out a blank report form and a notepad. He wanted to be ready to take down the necessary information and leave as soon as

Beth returned from the kitchen.

"I hope instant coffee is OK."

She set the steaming cup on a nearby stand before plopping down next to him.

"It's fine. What did you want to report stolen?"

"A bicycle. It was taken right out of the garage."

Luke breathed a sigh of relief. Finally he was getting somewhere.

"What's your full name?"

"Elizabeth Fullerton."

Fullerton. Luke mulled the name over. *Why did it sound familiar?*

"What does your husband do?"

"He's a councilman," she quietly replied.

"I thought I recognized the name," Luke said, relieved to hear the pie-eyed woman was the wife of a city official. He must have gotten the wrong impression about her.

"I'd better keep my voice down so I don't wake him." Luke pulled out his pen and prepared to take notes.

With watery eyes and a tortured look, the woman softly replied, "Oh, he's probably in bed somewhere...with someone... but he's not at home. He's out of state doing whatever government officials do when they think they can get away with it."

Luke didn't know what to say. He picked up his coffee and took a few sips.

"Mrs. Fullerton, you make a great cup of coffee."

It actually tasted like shit, but he wouldn't tell her that.

"Now, what kind of bicycle is it?"

"We can talk about that later. Call me Beth. Kick off your shoes and get comfortable." The woman's voice was low and inviting. She slid a little closer, her hand just inches from his leg.

"No thanks," Luke replied. "I'd better get this done and get back out there or my sergeant will come looking for me."

"Are you sure I couldn't interest you in something other than work?" She grinned seductively. "It must get lonely out there at night all by yourself. It gets awfully lonely for me."

Luke was getting more uncomfortable by the minute. He had no intention of having an affair with anyone, let alone the wife of a city official. But he had to be careful. If he made her mad, she might say he made a pass at her. No one would take the word of a lowly beat cop over the wife of a city official.

Luke took another sip of the shitty coffee and slowly set his cup down. He needed time to figure out how he was going to get out of this sticky situation without offending his host.

"I don't have time to get lonely." He began filling in the report form. "We keep really busy so I'd better hurry up and get this report done."

"You work too hard. You know what they say about all work and no play. You need to relax. Are you sure I can't get you a drink?" Beth flashed him an intimate smile.

"No thanks. Coffee is just fine." Luke picked up his cup and prepared to take another sip. It was empty. He didn't recall drinking it all.

"Can I get you some more coffee?" Beth asked.

"No thanks," he quickly replied. His stomach was already churning from the crap he just drank.

How was he going to explain to this woman that he wasn't interested in an affair without pissing her off? A woman scorned...

"Mrs. Fullerton...Beth...You are a very nice lady, and I thank you for the coffee and the conversation. But I need to get this report done and get back on the street. My wife will be worried if I have to work overtime and I'm late getting home. We've been married more than twenty years and she has her hands full raising our three kids. I try to help out as much as I can. I'm sure you understand."

Beth moved away and slowly got up. "The bicycle is in the alley," she whispered.

Luke rose to his feet. "Show me where and I'll get it for you."

The woman led him through the back yard to the alley where a bicycle was propped against the block wall.

"Whoever took your bike, didn't take it far," Luke said.

He wheeled it into the garage.

"Now, how about that for immediately solving a crime and returning the goods?" he joked.

Beth stood quietly, her face flushed with a beaten-down look of embarrassment.

Luke could sense the woman's discomfort. She had offered her most personal possession: her body, and there were no takers. He needed to find a way to soften the blow.

"I don't see the necessity for any kind of report since the property was recovered and no harm done. Do you?"

Beth's eyes gained some brightness. She looked at the officer as if seeing him for the first time. "No," she said. "I see no need for a report. Thank you."

"You're very welcome. Thank you for the coffee. That was a nice break," Luke said. He left the house and hurried down the walk. He was very relieved to be out of the house and out of reach of the lonely woman.

"You tell your wife she's a very lucky woman," Beth called.

Yeah, I'll be sure and tell my wife she's very lucky that I didn't jump into bed with the wife of a city official. Like hell I will. I can get into enough trouble with Emily accidentally. I'm not going to deliberately ask for it.

***

It was another long and sleepy autumn night. A full moon, occasionally dimmed by a scattering of lacy clouds, lit up the parking lots and side streets nearly as well as the streetlights.

It wasn't a good night to be a burglar. No burglar worth his salt would be out on a night like this. They liked the moonless nights. And if it was raining, so much the better. A good hard rain and a little wind muffled the sound of breaking glass or busted doors. Regardless of the weather, Luke always made sure the businesses in his area were secure.

After making his usual 2 a.m. stop at the donut shop, he headed north on 7th Street. The eastern side of his beat actually ended at Central Avenue, but he always made it a point to check the two taverns on the east side of 7th Street between Dunlap and Mountain View. Both appeared to be locked up tight. Their parking lots were empty. He swung a left on Mountain View, a left on Central, and a right on Hatcher.

There was one tavern on the south side of Hatcher just west of 7th Avenue, and two on the north side a few blocks farther west. One was a biker bar. All were occasional trouble spots.

It hadn't been that long ago since Sunnyslope was annexed into the city, so parts of the area were still pretty rowdy. Although the law required all taverns to close at 1 a.m., patrons sometimes hung around in the parking lots. Nearby residents had often complained of noisy fighting and an occasional gunshot long after the bars had closed.

Luke checked one of the taverns on the north side of the street. Everything looked secure. The parking lot was empty.

As he pulled up to the other one a few blocks farther west, he noticed a car parked in front of the building. No one was visible inside the vehicle. A quick check of the building revealed everything intact.

With his headlights on bright and his spotlight trained on the parked car, Luke slowly walked up to the vehicle and peered through the windows. A man appeared to be asleep on the front seat. A passed out drunk, no doubt. The back seat was empty.

Luke debated whether to let the man sleep it off, or wake him and see who he was and what he was doing there. He decided to run the plate. Maybe it was a stolen car.

He returned to his car and picked up the mic.

"Six-twenty-one."

"Six-twenty-one," the dispatcher acknowledged.

"Six-twenty-one. Can you run a plate for me?"

"10-4."

"Six-twenty-one. Arizona AMA-459."

"Standby."

Luke chuckled as he read the plate again. The police code for burglary was 459. The license plate was screaming, "*I am a burglar.*"

After several minutes, the dispatcher's voice once again broke the stillness of the night.

"Six-twenty-one, that plate is registered to a James Granger, 1189 E. Diane Street, Phoenix."

"10-4. Thanks," Luke replied.

"James Granger. James Granger," Luke repeated out loud. "Could it be Jimmy Granger, the safe burglar? Nah. He wouldn't be stupid enough to display a license plate that boasted about being a burglar, and then pass out in front of a tavern."

Luke walked up to the vehicle and again shone his flashlight through the windows to examine every inch of the interior. No weapons were in sight. He rapped on the window with his flashlight.

After a few hard taps, the man in the front seat pulled himself upright and rested his head on the steering wheel. He made no move to roll down the window or open the door.

Luke grasped the door handle and was surprised to find the door unlocked. He pulled it wide and stood quietly for a while in order to let the occupant see it was a cop who had awakened him.

"Rough night?" Luke quietly asked. His question was met with silence.

After getting a good look at the man, Luke determined it was not Jimmy Granger, the safe burglar. This man was a lot younger, although there was a strong resemblance.

"Is this your car?" he asked.

Still no response.

"May I see your driver's license?" Luke calmly asked.

The man turned to face Luke, his eyes watery and his mouth pulled tight. "You guys never give up, do you? You've got to be harassing someone all the time, even when they aren't doing anything. Well, take me to jail and get it over with." He extended his arms.

"Have you done something for which you should go to jail?" Luke asked.

The man scoffed. "Does that make a difference?"

"It does with me," Luke replied. "May I see your driver's license?"

"I don't have one."

"Well, how about some ID of some kind? Do you have

anything with your name on it?"

"No," came the reply.

"What's your name?" Luke asked.

"Jim Brown."

Luke Grinned. "Are you sure your name is James Brown?"

The man failed to answer.

"Is this your car?"

"No."

"Whose car is it?"

"A friend lent it to me."

"What's the friend's name?"

"I don't remember."

"Step out of the car," Luke ordered.

The young man did as directed.

Luke patted him down and led him to his patrol car. "Have a seat until I can get your identity and the owner of the car straightened out." Luke opened the back door and put the man inside. Since a heavy metal screen separated the front seat of the police car from the back, and the doors opened only from the outside, the prisoner was secured.

Luke returned to the young man's car and searched the interior. Under the front seat was a wallet. He opened it up to find a driver's license for nineteen-year-old Leland James Granger. It was obviously the young man Luke had just put in the back seat of his patrol car.

Granger was sitting quietly with his head down when Luke returned to his patrol car and picked up the mic.

"Six-twenty-one."

"Six-twenty-one," the dispatcher acknowledged.

"Six-twenty-one. Can you run a name for me?"

"10-4."

"Six-twenty-one. The name is Leland James Granger, white male. DOB 3-16-57."

"10-4. Standby."

While waiting for the information from the dispatcher, Luke again examined the driver's license in his hand. "Are you Leland James Granger?"

His question was met with silence.

"Are you Leland James Granger?" Luke repeated.

Again, no answer.

"Are you Jimmie Granger's son?"

Still no answer.

"That's his car you were in, isn't it?" Luke asked. "If it's his car, and you have permission to drive it, why won't you admit it and save yourself from all these questions?"

"Six-twenty-one." The dispatcher's voice interrupted.

"Six-twenty-one," Luke acknowledged.

"Six-twenty-one. We have an extensive record on James Leland Granger with a much older birthdate, but nothing on Leland James Granger."

"10-4. Thanks."

Luke got out and opened the back door of the patrol car. "Step out here," he said.

Granger stepped out and stood quietly, his head hanging.

"So what's going on," Luke asked. "Why not admit who you are? You don't have a record so you have nothing to fear from the police. And I doubt you planned to commit a crime driving a car around that says, I am a burglar." Luke had to chuckle again, just thinking about it.

Granger slowly lifted his head. "Would you admit you were the son of a criminal? Everywhere I go, I'm reminded that my father is a crook. Everybody thinks I'm one too, just because of my name."

"You can't help what your father does," Luke said. "I met your father in a restaurant once. He seemed to be a pretty nice guy. He even offered to buy me and my partner lunch. You know you can still love your father without loving the things he's done."

"That's easy for you to say. Your father probably hasn't done anything for you to be ashamed of. I have the same name.

I'm screwed before I can open my mouth to explain anything."

"Do you still live at home?"

"Yes."

"Where do you work?"

"I go to school full time."

"High school?"

"College."

"Who pays for that?"

"My father."

"What are you going to do when you finish college?"

Granger hesitated before answering. "I don't know. I haven't thought that far ahead."

"Have you ever considered becoming a cop?"

Granger eyed Luke suspiciously before answering. "Are you serious, or are you just screwing with me?"

"You have a clean record," Luke replied. "There's no reason why you couldn't be anything you wanted. The only thing stopping you is yourself. I think you would make a good cop. Your father has done some bad things, but he must have done something right raising you. You're nineteen years old with a clean record. Think about it."

A grimace followed by a slow smile spread across Granger's face. For the first time since Luke confronted him, he straightened up and looked Luke right in the eyes.

"Does your father know you have his car?" Luke asked.

"He knows," Granger said. "We got into our usual argument about him being a criminal so I left as usual. He's still my dad and he has a bad heart, so when I start losing my temper, I leave rather than getting him all worked up too. The cops might shoot and kill him some night, but I'm not going to be responsible for his death. I couldn't live with that."

"That's probably a smart thing to do," Luke said. He handed Granger back his driver's license and wallet. "Now that you've had a chance to cool off, go home and get some sleep. Things always look better in the daylight."

Granger climbed into his car. Luke watched him drive away. He felt sorry for the young man. *Sometimes kids turn out to be decent human beings in spite of their parents.* The thought brought a smile to his lips. He felt as if he had accomplished something. Maybe the words he had spoken to Leland James Granger would spark a sense of respect for his father and set the young man on the road to success.

Luke glanced at his watch. 3:10 a.m. He'd spent a lot more time with the Granger kid than he thought. He had the bar to check on the south side of the street and then he'd have checked every business in his beat area.

He pulled into the tavern parking lot and swung around the back. Everything looked OK, but something didn't feel right. He shut the engine off and sat quietly, listening for any sound.

He hadn't waited long when he heard a loud crash from inside. Luke stepped out of his police car and approached the back door. It looked intact. His hand was on the door knob when a figure suddenly appeared at the corner of the building. Luke reached for his gun.

"Hey. Don't shoot. I'm one of the good guys." Dennis Creech had a grin on his face.

"What the hell are you doing sneaking around? I damn near shot you," Luke growled.

"I was driving by and saw you pull in so I thought I'd drop by and say hello," Creech said. "Besides, you need a backup. I took the liberty of calling a couple of other units, including the wagon. They should be here shortly."

"What the hell for? We don't even know if we have anything or not. All I heard was a noise. For all I know, it might have been you," Luke said.

"I told radio to contact the manager and get him down here. I think there's more going on inside than we can handle," Creech said. "We'll wait for backup."

Luke couldn't explain it, but he suddenly felt the same. "I

checked the exterior and I didn't see any sign of a break-in, but something is going on in there," Luke said.

The wagon was the first to arrive, followed shortly by two other units. The bar manager pulled in right behind them. He hurried over to the back door where Luke and Creech were standing.

"What's going on?" he asked. "I don't see any break-in."

"You got here fast," Luke said.

"I worked late cleaning the place up. I haven't been to bed yet. I only live two blocks away," the manager said.

"We think there's someone inside," Luke explained. "Is there supposed to be someone staying in there at night?"

"Hell no," the manager said. "No one should be in there."

"So you called a half dozen officers over here when you don't even know if someone is in there?" one of the burly wagon officers groused.

"There's someone in there," Creech quietly said. "I suggest you be prepared for a fight."

The wagon officer scoffed as the manager turned the key in the lock and swung the door open.

Luke was intent on being the first one through the door. It was his beat. He should be the one to spearhead the operation. But Creech blocked his entry until all the other officers were inside. "Don't be in such a hurry to get your ass kicked," he said.

The first thing Luke noticed was the air vent broken loose from the ceiling and lying in a tangled mess of twisted metal on the floor. As he was trying to make sense of it all, a medium size man, bleeding from cuts to his face and arms, crawled out from the debris and stood defiantly, his arms at his side. The suspect had apparently removed the swamp cooler on the roof and crawled into the vent. His weight was too much for the aging metal straps that held it to the ceiling. Luke had run across scenes like this before. But in those instances, the burglar was long gone before the police arrived.

Luke got a sudden chill. It wasn't like the chill from an Iowa winter that penetrated his clothing and froze his skin. This one started on the inside and worked its way throughout his body. It was the chill that comes with knowing you are standing face to face with evil.

"Turn around and put your hands behind your back," one of the wagon officers ordered.

Instead of following commands to turn around, the suspect moved forward, his bloody face sporting a crooked grin.

The wagon officers were the first to pounce on him. They each grabbed a bloody arm and attempted to force it behind the suspect's back. The suspect swung his arms. Both officers went flying.

Luke leaped forward, knocking the suspect off balance. Two other back up officers jumped on the man, along with the wagon officers who had regained their feet and returned to the fray. Luke tried to grab onto the man's arm, but the blood from a serious cut made it too slippery to hang onto. Creech nudged him aside as the four other officers managed to subdue the man and place him in cuffs. When he continued to resist, they hogtied him and placed him face down on the floor.

Luke staggered over to a bar stool and sat down. He felt drained, but it was more of an emotional drain rather than physical. He also felt dirty. Like he needed to take a shower and scrub himself clean.

He went to the restroom and scrubbed his hands and arms and washed his face. He still felt dirty. He repeated the process. It didn't make him feel any better.

Other officers came in to get washed up. "What the hell did you get us into?" one of them complained. "It felt like I was in the fight of my life."

"And he was just a scrawny run of the mill burglar," another officer said. "Either I'm getting soft, or crooks are getting tougher."

Luke didn't comment. He could feel the force of evil

emanating from the man. In all his days, and in all of the criminals he'd arrested, he had never met someone whom he considered to be pure evil. Until tonight, that is.

The officers carried the suspect out to the wagon and threw him aboard, still hogtied. Let him bounce around back there on the way to the hospital. They had to get him patched up before the jail would accept him. Maybe the ride would soften him up so they'd be able to book him without another fight.

After obtaining the necessary information for his report, Luke waited until the place was secure and the manager was pulling out of the parking lot before turning to Dennis Creech. There were a number of important questions he wanted to ask the detective. How did he know there was someone inside the tavern? And how did he know the suspect would put up such a hard fight. More importantly than that, why did he protect Luke from becoming too involved in subduing the man? But as usual, they were stuck somewhere in his brain.

"Thanks Dennis," Luke said. "Who are you? What are you? How…?"

Creech grinned. "I just learned to use my intuition. You will too. Nothing more to it than that. But someday, I might just tell you all about it. Catch you later." He walked to his car and drove off, leaving Luke with mixed emotions and a whole lot of unanswered questions.

What the hell was Creech doing out at this time of night? He surely wasn't following up on an investigation at three o'clock in the morning. And what was the deal with him making sure Luke didn't become too involved in the fight?

Luke needed coffee. He crawled into his patrol car and headed for the donut shop. Try as he might, he couldn't figure Dennis Creech out. He was a constant pain in the ass when they were on the same squad, and yet, he always seemed to be Luke's protector whenever trouble arose. Maybe he's really an angel. Luke shook his head, disgusted with the thought. "Yeah, and maybe he's just a pain in the ass."

There were a great many puzzling things in Luke's life. But this was one of the biggest. Maybe one day, he'd figure it out, but right now he had something more important to consider–what kind of donut to have with his coffee. He grinned as he pulled up to the donut shop and slowly made his way inside.

CHAPTER TWELVE

It was nearing 4:30 a.m. on a Sunday when Luke pulled up to a group of paper delivery boys on Central Avenue. They gathered in the same location each morning to bundle newspapers before delivery. Their bicycles were strewn on the ground around them.

Luke had made it a point to stop by each morning. He always marveled at their work ethic. It took a lot of effort to get up that early and he wanted to make sure they didn't run into any trouble. In addition, he found them to be a good source of information. They provided him with extra eyes and ears for any criminal activity.

"Good morning gentlemen," Luke said. "How is everything this morning?"

"OK," one of the boys replied while folding newspapers

and stuffing them into a pouch on his bike.

"Anything going on?" he asked.

"Nah," one boy replied.

Luke was about to pull away and continue his patrol when one of the boys said, "I thought I saw someone on the roof of the restaurant across the street when I first got here, but when I looked closer no one was there. Maybe I was seeing things."

The Stine and Sirloin sat directly across from where the boys were folding papers.

"OK, thanks. I'll take a look," Luke said.

He drove across the street and checked the exterior of the building, but found nothing out of place. Still, there had been a number of roof jobs lately. He decided to check it out. He asked radio to send the paddy wagon. It carried a ladder.

Twenty minutes later, the wagon pulled up. "You guys are a pain in the ass," one of the wagon officers groused. "We've been too busy to even stop for coffee. And now you want to waste our time because some paper boy thought he saw something?"

"It may turn out to be nothing. But better safe than sorry," Luke responded. He pulled the ladder from the roof of the wagon and propped it up against the building.

"I'll go up and check it out," Luke said. He crawled slowly up and peered cautiously over the lip of the roof.

As with many commercial buildings, the restaurant had a flat roof with a two foot lip. Several swamp-coolers were spaced out across the roof.

Evaporative coolers were prevalent throughout the area, not only because they were efficient, except during the monsoon season, they were also cheap to run.

Seeing no activity, Luke scaled the lip of the roof and shone his flashlight around the area. That same annoying voice in his head told him to be careful. Wait for a backup. But nothing appeared out of place. He ignored the warning.

He made his way to an area nearest the alley and spotted a light coming up through the roof. As he got closer, he could see a large hole with an acetylene torch and tank nearby. The tip of a ladder protruded from the hole.

He pulled his gun and eased closer to the hole. The burglars must still be in the restaurant. He carefully examined the scene below, but saw and heard no one.

"Drop the guns and get your hands up," a voice behind him yelled.

He spun around to see two men with guns pointed at him. They froze for a few seconds before laying their guns down and raising their hands. One of the wagon officers had them at gunpoint.

After getting the suspects down and safely into the wagon, Luke thanked the officer who had saved his bacon.

"It was lucky for me you followed me up the ladder," Luke said. "I didn't even see them. They must have been hiding behind a *swamp-cooler*. Damn! That was too close for comfort."

"You can thank some detective. He appeared out of nowhere and told me to get my ass up that ladder. He chewed me out for letting you go up there alone. Guess he was right," the wagon officer said.

"Who was it? Where is he now?" Luke glanced around at the numerous police cars and patrol officers milling around the area.

"I don't know," the wagon officer responded. "He was gone when we came down."

"Well, whoever it was, I probably owe *him* my life, as well as *you*," Luke said. He turned to see a newspaper reporter approaching.

"Are you the one who captured the burglars?" the reporter asked.

"No, I was just an innocent bystander," Luke said. He clasped the wagon officer on the shoulder. "This is the hero right here."

Luke got in his car and headed for the station. He had a

lengthy report to write and a short time until shift change. He needed a bite to eat, but he would settle for a good cup of coffee. He had escaped another close call. The voice in his head had warned him, but once again he refused to accept it. Maybe it was because he was still sane enough to realize something like that was impossible. People who heard voices ended up in the nut house. If he gave in and accepted the reality of it, he might be one of them.

He wondered who the detective was that ordered the wagon officer up the ladder. Whoever it was, Luke probably owed him his life. If he had taken seriously, however, the cautionary voice that warned him to be careful, he wouldn't have been in that dangerous situation to begin with. When was he going to learn to heed the silent warnings? After he was dead?

***

The months passed. It was late in March. Desert flowers were popping out and orange blossoms were spreading their heavenly fragrance throughout the area. Luke was back on second shift. It would be less than a week until day shift would roll around again. Although second shift was often busy, he hadn't run across any life threatening situations. Things like that always seemed to run in spurts. It was either quiet for a period of time, or all hell was busting loose. There never seemed to be a middle ground. He'd been on shift two for nearly two months, and there was nothing but routine calls.

It was nearing shift change when the call came out.

"Six-twenty-one?"

Luke reluctantly picked up the mic. "Six-twenty-one."

"Six-twenty-one, check welfare. It will be the trailer park on the northwest corner of Cave Creek and Hatcher. Space number eleven. A Mister Guy Turnbow. His daughter lives out of state. He lives alone and doesn't have a phone, but he always calls his daughter from a pay phone once a week on the same day and at the same time. He should have called last night. She is concerned something might have happened to him."

"Six-twenty-one, what do I tell him if he's there?"

"Six-twenty-one, just tell him to call his daughter."

"10-4."

Luke was glad the address was near the station. He was tired and didn't feel like working overtime.

The trailer park had been there long before Sunnyslope became a part of the city. Since it had been grandfathered in, it wasn't subject to city code. Luke had gotten calls there before. It was a jumble of old and dilapidated metal boxes that once passed for mobile homes. They were clustered together like a hobo camp.

It was hard to imagine any of them ever being mobile.

Family fight calls in there were the worst. The trailers were so small there wasn't room to move around. If someone was going to fight, they were on you before you were ready. But this was just a simple welfare check. There shouldn't be a problem.

He wound his way through the maze of narrow roads, and after a few rounds, came to space 11, wedged into a far corner of the court. The house was dark. A makeshift clothesline that sagged in the middle, stretched the length of the trailer. Several ragged shirts and denims hung inches from the ground. A beat up Ford pickup with a flat tire was sitting in the driveway. It provided the finishing touch; an exclamation point to the scene of abject poverty.

"Well, it looks like daddy is home," Luke mocked.

"Six-twenty-one, I'm 97."

"10-4," dispatch acknowledged.

He parked behind the Ford and sat quietly for a minute. It seemed ridiculous to send the police just to ask a relative to call home. But he was a public servant. His job was to serve the public. Maybe he should have checked with the dispatcher to see if he should deliver a bottle of milk and a dozen eggs as well.

Luke grabbled his flashlight and reluctantly climbed out of his patrol car. He shone his light inside the pickup as he walked by. It was empty. He flashed his light across the windows of the trailer in the hopes that someone inside would see it and come to the door. They didn't.

Several raps on the door with his flashlight failed to rouse anyone. He walked around the trailer, shining his light in the windows. Drawn curtains on some, and aluminum foil on others, prevented a view of the interior.

"Dammit," he muttered. "Wake up in there. It's late. I wanta go home."

He checked with the occupants of the closest trailer to see if they had seen or heard from Mr. Turnbow.

A toothless woman with a tattered dress came to the door.

"I'm Officer Canfield," Luke said. "Have you seen Mr. Turnbow recently?"

The old woman stared at Luke, but said nothing.

"Have you seen Mr. Turnbow recently?" he loudly repeated.

"What's he done?" the woman asked.

"His daughter is worried about him. I'm just here to see if he's all right. Have you seen him?"

"I don't pay 'tention to no one 'round here," the woman said.

"Okay," Luke said.

The woman closed the door and switched off the lights inside.

"Yeah, you don't pay 'tention. That's why you shut the lights off. Not because you want to see what I'm going to do without me knowing you're watching me," Luke mumbled.

He returned to space 11 and banged harder on the door.

No answer.

He turned the door knob. The door creaked open. He shone his light in.

"Hello!" Luke shouted. "Phoenix police."

No answer.

He swung the door wide and stood waiting for a voice to ask him what the hell he thought he was doing, coming into a man's home without being invited.

Hearing no sound, Luke stepped inside. It was a typical cramped interior, just like all the rest in this little slice of hell. There was a musty smell of soiled shag carpet that most old trailers held that Luke had been in. Some dirty dishes in the sink were host to several cockroaches that scurried to find cover from Luke's flashlight.

He found the light switch and flipped it on. Nothing happened. The place was obviously without electricity.

Luke slowly made his way back to the lone bedroom. His

flashlight in one hand and the other on his gun.

The first thing he saw was a man's bare feet sticking straight up.

"Hello," Luke called. "Mr. Turnbow? Phoenix police."

No answer.

He cautiously peeked around the corner. His light caught the flicker of an eyelid. He quickly pulled his head back.

"Sorry to disturb you, Mr. Turnbow," he said. "Your daughter asked us to check on you. Are you all right?"

Mr. Turnbow didn't answer.

Maybe he had a stroke and can't speak.

Luke stepped into the bedroom, shone his flashlight on Mr. Turnbow's face, and cringed. What he thought was the flicker of an eyelid was actually a cockroach doing wheelies on the man's eyeball. Mr. Turnbow was obviously dead.

He didn't appear to have been dead for more than a few hours. The body hadn't yet started to putrefy and there were no flies on the windows.

There were some house calls Luke had been on where the body hadn't been discovered for several days. Flies were so thick on the outside of the windows it looked like the shutters were closed. The windows were clear with this one. Still, he was glad it wasn't the middle of summer. Heat hastened decay, and dead body odor was one smell he couldn't tolerate without vomiting. One whiff was all it took.

After taking one last look around, Luke returned to his patrol car and picked up the mic.

"Six-twenty-one."

"Six-twenty-one," the dispatcher answered.

"Six-twenty-one, there appears to be a 901-H at this address. Better roll the detectives."

"10-4," dispatch replied.

Luke placed the mic back in its cradle and glanced at his watch. It was already past quitting time. "Well, hell," he said aloud. "So much for going home on time. Why the hell couldn't the man's daughter have called a little earlier?"

He reluctantly pulled out a report form. It would take some time before the detectives could get out there from downtown. He might as well write his report while he waited.

He suddenly felt guilty for his thoughts and for his sarcastic comments. A woman in another state was worried about her father. All she wanted was for him to call home. Instead of a phone call, she was going to get a visit from some cop telling her that her father is never going to call because he's dead. And Luke was resenting a simple call to check welfare. He should be ashamed of himself.

He was.

***

Emily Canfield finished her housework and glanced around to make sure she hadn't missed anything. Luke was at work, the kids were in school, and she had the rest of the day to herself. She should be grateful to have some free time. But her head was about to explode from worry. She worried about the kids. She worried about Luke. What would she do if he got hurt and could no longer work? She had never worked outside the home. Her skills as a mother and housekeeper wouldn't get her very far in the outside world. How could she support herself and three kids? She became angry with herself. Thoughts like that wouldn't do her or anyone else any good.

Her hand shook as she poured herself a cup of coffee and retreated to the family room. Burying her nose in a good book might relieve her anxiety. She never liked hearing about real life police activity, but she enjoyed fictional mysteries and detective stories.

The doorbell was an annoying interruption. Probably a salesman. It was strange that Skippy didn't bark. He usually raised a fuss if anyone approached the front door. But he remained sprawled on the floor, his tail wagging furiously. She had never seen such strange behavior. She hoped he wasn't getting sick. They couldn't afford another vet bill.

She hesitated. If she refused to answer the door, the caller might go away. No. It might be important. One of the kids, maybe, or it could be that Luke had gotten hurt.

She slowly opened the door. The first thing she noticed was the gun on his hip. But he was in plain clothes. It must be a detective.

"Is it Luke?" she asked breathlessly.

"No, Luke is fine. You probably don't remember me. I'm Dennis Creech. We met at a squad party a few years ago. We met again when I brought your daughter home."

Emily breathed a sigh of relief. "Thank God," she whispered. "You scared me. I thought something had happened to Luke."

"No. He's fine. You don't have to worry about him. I doubt anything will ever happen to him," Creech said.

Emily eyed the detective carefully. "I wish I was as sure as you. He always seems to get himself in dangerous situations."

"Yeah, but he always comes out unscathed," Creech countered.

"What is it then?" Emily asked. "It isn't one of the kids, is it?" Her breath caught in her throat at the thought.

"No, the kids are fine. I was just in the area and thought I would drop by and say hello. I also wanted to check on Amy." Creech's face lit up with a broad smile. It was like the sun peaking over the horizon on an early summer morning. It lit up the entire doorway.

Emily was caught up in the glow. The brooding thoughts she had experienced before the doorbell rang were now replaced with a feeling of peace and contentment. Everything was going to be all right. She had nothing more to worry about.

"The last time I was here, Amy was late getting home from school and you had a little problem with that. Do you remember me being here?"

Emily suddenly realized she was still standing in the doorway. "Of course. Come in. I guess I was too befuddled at the time to thank you properly. I'm glad you stopped by. Thank you again for seeing Amy safely home and for coming to my rescue so promptly. She has come straight home ever since."

She led the way into the kitchen and motioned to the table. "Have a seat. Would you like a cup of coffee?"

"No thanks," Creech replied. "Never could stand the stuff. I don't see how people can get it down."

"I've wondered the same thing myself," Emily chuckled.

"Although I do have a cup from time to time. I'd much rather have a soda, but I figured coffee was less fattening."

Creech nodded agreement. "You're probably right about that."

"So, you're a detective." Emily said. "At the rate Luke is going, he'll probably still be chasing shoplifters when you become chief."

"I'll never go any higher," Creech said. "I'm satisfied to be where I am right now. But don't sell your husband short. He doesn't even realize it himself, but he has more insight than people give him credit for. He'll probably make sergeant before too long."

Emily gave her guest a quizzical glance. "I find your comments surprising. I had the impression you two never really got along."

Creech grinned. "Yeah, well, we have a lot more in common than he realizes."

After a few more minutes of idle chatter, Creech rose from the table. "Well, I'd better be going. I enjoyed our chat. You might not want to mention that I stopped by. I'm supposed to be working instead of socializing with attractive women. You wouldn't want to get me in trouble now, would you?" he grinned.

"No. I certainly wouldn't want to get you in trouble," Emily smiled as the detective headed for the door.

After he left, she returned to the family room, reliving in her mind the conversation she'd just had with Detective Creech. How was it that he spoke so highly of her husband when Luke had nothing good to say about him? And what made him so sure that Luke would be OK, and that he would soon be promoted? She knew he was on the promotional list, but…

"Idle talk," she said aloud as she picked up a magazine and reached for her coffee. "Just idle talk."

One question lingered in her mind, however: *Why did she always feel so much better emotionally after being in the presence of Dennis Creech?*

CHAPTER THIRTEEN

More than six years had passed since Luke joined the Phoenix police department. He liked working the streets as a uniformed patrol officer and he had no desire to become a supervisor. But as the kids got older, there were more bills for clothes and dentists and a myriad of school activities. The expenditures never seemed to slow.

Out of desperation, Luke took the sergeant's test and made the promotion list. But the list only lasted for two years. It would soon run out. There wasn't much hope that he would make it this time around. That meant he would have to start the process all over again.

He'd had a number of different supervisors since his transfer to Sunnyslope. Some he'd liked better than others, but

Luke learned something from each. He tucked away all of the positive attributes in the back of his mind in case the day ever came when he was a supervisor. But he never forgot the negative ones either. He would make sure not to emulate them.

It was a Thursday, Luke's first day back to work after his regular two days off, when he received the memo. He read the words over and over before they finally sunk in:

Effective Monday, June 9th, 1969, you will be promoted to the rank of sergeant. Please report to the Chief's office at 2 p.m. for the promotion process.

You will be assigned to the Patrol Bureau, District 8. Report to Lieutenant Jerry Harvy prior to that date for your work-hours and assignment.

Report to the Information Bureau within one week of your promotion to get your picture taken in your sergeant's insignia.

Congratulations!

At the bottom was the chief's bold signature.

PART FOUR – THE SERGEANT

"Destiny has two ways of crushing us – by refusing our wishes and by fulfilling them." – Henri Frederic Amiel, Swiss writer *(1821-1881)*

CHAPTER FOURTEEN

Pat's Cafe was nearly deserted except for an elderly couple munching toast in a booth by the door and a straggly-haired young man at the end of the counter. The breakfast rush had passed and the lunch crowd hadn't trickled in yet. It was a perfect time for Sergeant Luke Canfield to stop for coffee and complete some paperwork.

He took the last swallow of coffee and placed his cup at the far side of the table, away from the papers spread out before him. It wouldn't do for a coffee ring to show up on anything that his lieutenant had to sign off on.

Luke gathered up the probationer's monthly progress reports he had just completed, arranged them in alphabetical order inside a manila folder, and slid the folder into his briefcase.

All seven were due tomorrow. He was thankful the other five members of his squad were veterans. Evaluations for them were annual.

The aging wall-clock behind the counter caught Luke's attention. Ten thirty-seven. He'd been in the coffee shop longer than intended. In fact, he shouldn't have been there at all. It wasn't his area. But it was on the main road back to his squad area after attending a meeting downtown, so it was a convenient place to stop for a cup.

He could have completed all paperwork in his patrol car where he would be available for calls, but radio traffic was light this Thursday morning. Besides, Pat's was a lot more comfortable and a hell of a lot cooler.

All the while he was working on his reports, Luke kept an eye on the straggly-haired young man at the end of the counter. The man had gotten up once to go to the restroom and walked right by the uniformed sergeant without as much as a glance. That was suspicious in itself. Everyone stared at a police officer. Everyone, that is, except those who didn't want the officer staring back.

Nearly eight years on the job provided more than enough experience to spot a drug user. The hair often gave them away, and this one's hair was screaming, "I'm a junky!"

The furtive movements of the young man's head from the front window and back to the kitchen, gave all the earmarks of someone up to no good. He wasn't even pretending to eat or drink. A glass of water sat nearby, but he hadn't touched it. A visual scan revealed nothing that looked like a concealed weapon, but it wasn't always easy to tell.

Luke couldn't understand why the restaurant employees seemed so nonchalant about the situation. Pat came out from the kitchen on several occasions, but she never even looked his way. Neither did the waitress who kept filling the sergeant's cup.

Is everyone in here asleep? Luke argued with himself whether to ignore the man or check him out. *They'll damn sure wake up when he pulls a gun and robs the place.*

He decided to take some action. He couldn't just sit there and do nothing. Luke hoisted his lanky frame up from the booth and fished in his pocket for some change. Cops weren't charged for coffee at most places, but he always left fifty cents. It was up to the waitress to choose what to do with it.

Luke had only been in the restaurant a few times. He knew Pat when he saw her. But he wasn't familiar with any of her employees, or the patrons who are usually as much of a fixture as the help.

He intercepted the waitress on her way to pour some coffee

for the couple in the front booth.

"Has anyone noticed the guy sitting at the end of the counter?" he asked.

"What about him?" the waitress responded.

"Have you seen him in here before?"

"Of course," the waitress replied. "That's Pat's son. Why?"

"I just thought he looked familiar, but I couldn't place him. I must have seen him in here before." Luke turned his head to hide his surprise.

"Damn. That was a close one," he muttered on his way out the door. "Good thing I didn't do anything before I asked about the guy. Pat's son. Who knew?"

Heat from the asphalt felt as if Luke was walking on hot coals. It radiated through the legs of his heavy wool uniform, causing rivulets of sweat to trickle down his back. He hurried to his car parked under a tree at the far end of the lot. It was summer in Phoenix, and any shade, no matter how meager, was a welcome respite from the relentless sun.

He learned the hard way about taking precautions from the sun just two days after arriving in the Valley. Amy had suffered second degree burns on her butt and the back of her legs from a trip down a metal slide. Stories like that were unheard of in Iowa. But in Phoenix they were common place.

It was like opening an oven when he threw open the car door. After letting the initial blast of heat escape from the interior, he climbed in and hurriedly started the engine. The air conditioner roared to life, laboring to reduce the interior temperature to a bearable level. He sat quietly for a few minutes, hesitant to touch the steering wheel until it got a little cooler.

As he swung out of the parking lot and headed northwest on Grand Avenue, he thought about his near mistake. He was thankful he hadn't acted on his first impulse of slamming young *Straggly-Hair* against the counter and patting him down.

"No more free coffee, I would guess." Luke chuckled.

Just goes to show. Things aren't always what they seem.

Luke was proof of that. He still found it amusing when he thought of his present role. He didn't look like the posters depicting a police officer, and most of the time he didn't act like one. He didn't have that *"I'm a cop and you're not"* attitude that many officers presented. He looked and acted more like a farmer, and that was the way he approached police work. Farm boys weren't told how to do something. They were assigned a task and it was up to them how best to carry it out. Failure was never an option.

Because of his calm, quiet, almost shy demeanor, Luke was often underestimated. But that was the way he liked it. People were always surprised when he performed better than expected.

He had barely made it back to his squad area when his reverie was broken by a bone chilling *hot tone* from the police radio. The ominous wail always preceded an emergency transmission. He'd heard it hundreds of times before, but it still sent chills down his spine, along with a surge of adrenaline.

"All units, shots fired, 4400 block of North 57th Drive." The dispatcher sounded calm. But then, she always did, regardless of the type of call.

Luke admired her for that. He had great respect for the dispatchers. The officers may have been the responders, but the voices behind the calls were their guardian angels.

Luke reached for the mic. As far as radio knew, he was still at the main station. "Eighty-one en route," he said as he turned west on Indian School Road and headed in the direction of the call.

Luke knew some of his officers would get to the scene before him. That's the way it should be. It was their beat. But he was the area sergeant and he had to get there before his lieutenant. It didn't matter how far away, or what else was going on. The sergeant was always supposed to get to the scene ahead of his boss.

He learned early on that Lieutenant Harvy was a strict, by-the-book supervisor. To Harvy, everything was either black or white. Gray didn't exist.

Harvy wasn't a particularly big man. He was only about 5'10" and 175 pounds. But he had an air about him that made him seem bigger. Some called it a smug attitude. His spit shined shoes, short black hair, and clean shaven face complemented his no-nonsense military bearing. It fit right in with his obsession to follow policy.

Talk among the sergeants was that he would have made an ideal German SS officer during WW-II. If policy dictated, he could easily have carried out the order of genocide without a second thought.

But while others found it difficult to work for the man, Luke found it easy. Although his lieutenant was inflexible when it came to following policy, he was a knowledgeable and competent supervisor. He was also consistent. Luke could work for anyone who didn't change the ground rules to suit the occasion. Besides that, he liked his boss.

Luke arrived on the scene with Lieutenant Harvy close behind. Officers had already cordoned off each end of the block in which the suspect's house was located.

Both supervisors followed protocol and parked their police cars out of the line of fire. True to form, Harvy parked on the right hand side of the street, within the legal eighteen inches from the curb. Luke was less concerned about minor regulations. He parked facing traffic, on the same side of the street as the suspected shots had been fired. He wanted his car as close as possible in case he needed the radio or the first-aid kit.

Luke shook his head as he recalled his earlier days in Phoenix. Less than four years ago, the area was an orange grove with fruit laden trees that stretched as far as the eye could see. Now, the land held rows of single level homes that stood nearly as close together as the trees they'd replaced. Each Bermuda grass lawn hosted two evenly-spaced mulberry trees. Their long, spindly branches stretched out and up as though surrendering to the desert sun. A carport, wide enough for a pickup as well as the family car, was the only separation between properties.

As they walked up to the crime-scene tape blocking the street, Officer Chris Pullin greeted them. His short, stocky body didn't fit the image normally associated with a Phoenix Police Officer. It was rumored he had put his socks on over a pair of shower clogs in order to comply with the five foot-nine height requirement. His wide mouth, sandy hair, and flushed face did nothing to improve his appearance. He always looked as if he'd just crawled out of bed after sleeping all night with his clothes on.

Even though his uniform was clean, it was ill-fitting. Luke had previously attempted to correct Pullin's appearance, but finally realized it wasn't the uniform that needed fixing, it was the officer's misshapen body. So Luke resigned himself to that fact and let things be.

He noticed his lieutenant giving Pullin the once-over. But this was not the time to discuss an officer's appearance. There was a lot more at stake than a wrinkled uniform.

"What do we have?" Luke asked as they approached the officer.

"A man is firing a gun inside his house about halfway down the block on the east side of the street." Pullin pointed to the house in question. "He hasn't hit anyone yet, but according to a neighbor, he fired a lot of shots. They say he's a Vietnam vet and he has a history of shooting off guns. The neighbor I spoke with said he'd heard gunshots around midnight a few nights ago and suspected it was the same man."

"Have you made contact with the suspect?" Luke asked as he and Lieutenant Harvy ducked under the barrier tape and started up the street towards the house.

"No," Pullin said. "He doesn't have a phone. He borrowed the neighbor's phone whenever he needed to call someone. They say he lives alone and is believed to be the only one in the house. I thought it best if we just contain him and wait until a supervisor was on the scene before attempting to make contact. I and Officer

Beltser went through the alley and notified the home owners in the line of fire to stay inside and away from all doors and windows that fronted the street."

"Good decision," Luke said. He looked at his lieutenant as if to say, *I told you so.*

"Looks like you've done a good job isolating the situation. Let's go see what the man has to say," Luke added as he started up the sidewalk.

"Maybe we'd better evacuate the nearby homes before we go any further," Lieutenant Harvy said.

"How about if we hold off on that for now," Luke said. "Let me get up to the house and assess the situation first. We may cause casualties if we try to move people around while the suspect is shooting."

"OK," Harvy said. "But we don't want to wait too long."

As they approached the house, the sound of a large dog's incessant barking was heard coming from the interior, punctuated by intermittent blasts from a handgun.

"Sounds like the Fourth of July," Luke commented in an attempt to lighten the situation.

The officers made their way to the front door, thankful for the cement block construction of the homes in the area.

"Make sure you don't stand in front of the door," Luke

cautioned Officer Pullin.

When everyone was in position, Luke reached over and pounded his fist on the door below the knob. Two shots blasted through the door near the top. Chips of wood sprayed the area.

"That's why you never stand directly in front of a door when you knock, no matter what kind of call you're on," Luke pointed out to Officer Pullin. "In this case, you might not have been hit by a bullet, but you could have been hit in the eye by wood chips."

Pullin nodded. "I think I can get over to a side window where I can get a shot at him if need be." He started to move to the side of the house.

"No," Luke said. He motioned the officer back to his original position. "Let's not forget this man is a veteran who risked his life in the service of his country. I'm sure he's been shot at in Vietnam and managed to survive, at least physically. We sure don't want to take his life now if we can possibly avoid it. His shots were aimed high. If he really wanted to hurt someone, he'd have aimed a lot lower. As far as I'm concerned, this man is a hero and this is his house. We'll only use deadly force as a last resort."

Lieutenant Harvy voiced his approval. "We certainly don't want to shoot him if it can be avoided. We may have to wait him out."

Luke needed to come up with a better plan. It could take days for the shooter to exit peacefully, and they were far too busy to tie up several officers for that length of time.

"Hello in there," he yelled through the bullet-riddled door. "I'm Sergeant Canfield of the Phoenix Police Department. I need to talk with you."

"Go away," came a hoarse, guttural response.

Luke pretended not to hear. "What? I can't hear a word you're saying with that dog barking," he yelled. "Lock the dog in the bathroom and then come back to the door so I can hear what you're saying."

After repeated attempts to talk the man into locking his dog away, the subject finally complied.

"Go away," the man yelled after returning to the door.

"I still can't hear you through this heavy door," Luke shouted. "Get in front of the door and speak through the keyhole so I can hear what you're saying."

"Go away," the man screamed.

The words were barely out of the man's mouth when Luke kicked the door next to the knob with such force that the door flew off its hinges, knocking the man down with the door on top of him.

Luke followed the door as it went down, kneeling on

top of it with the gunman restrained beneath. The shooter's outstretched arm was pinned helplessly under the mangled door. The weapon that was so deadly a few minutes earlier was easily retrieved from the suspect's grasp.

After the suspect was handcuffed and the house was cleared of any additional occupants, Pullin led him out to a waiting paddy wagon. The gun was tagged, bagged, and handed over to the wagon officers for impounding as evidence.

"I don't like to put him in jail if he's truly a veteran," Luke told the wagon officers, "but we have no choice but to book him for discharging a weapon in the city limits as well as assault with a deadly weapon. Maybe by locking him up, he'll get some mental help when he goes before a judge. Treat him gently," he cautioned the wagon officers.

"We always do Sarge," one of the wagon officers called back as they pulled away from the curb.

Luke notified dispatch to have Animal Control pick up the dog that was still locked in the bathroom. He also asked for City Services to come out and secure the house.

After taking one last look around to make sure he hadn't forgotten anything, Luke joined Lieutenant Harvy, who had already left the house and was waiting on the street. Luke called Officer Pullin over to where he and the lieutenant were standing.

"You did a good job with this situation, Chris. You had everything well in hand. Good work. Make sure you notify the neighbors that it's safe to come out now. You'll have to stand by here at the house until Animal Control shows up. Also, make sure City Services fixes the door and the house is secure before you leave. You should have time to write your report while you're waiting."

Luke always made it a point to praise when appropriate and train when it wasn't. The words of praise were especially meaningful because they were given in the presence of the lieutenant. Luke smiled as Pullin walked across the street to notify the neighbors that all was safe. He looked lighter on his feet. His stride was more confident.

"Well, he probably feels better after you commended him, but he sure doesn't look any better," Lieutenant Harvy said before heading for his car.

As he prepared to drive away, the lieutenant looked back at his sergeant. "That was a good job," he said. "I'm not sure about the method you used, but everything worked out all right, so I guess it was the right one."

Luke nodded and got into his car. As soon as he was seated, he reached into his briefcase and pulled out his supervisor journal. The officer's performance rating was soon due and Luke wanted to make sure he made an entry while everything was still fresh in his mind.

Officer Pullin did a good job in securing the scene of a Vietnam vet who was firing a gun inside his house. All preliminary work was done by the time I arrived and he had things well in hand.

Luke returned the journal to his briefcase and headed for the station. He had a good deal of paperwork to catch up on before the next major incident.

He didn't have long to wait. Less than a mile up the road was a vehicle parked haphazardly against the curb. A man standing by the open back door of the late model Chrysler was waving his arms wildly and yelling at someone in the back seat. Luke stopped behind the car, careful to keep his vehicle between him and the man by the Chrysler.

"Not another damn family fight," Luke muttered.

He notified radio of his location and plate number of the Chrysler before getting out of his patrol car and walking slowly over, ready for anything. Family fights were dreaded by most cops. They were too unpredictable. People become irrational when angry and there is nothing like a conflict between a man and woman to stoke that anger. The appearance of a cop sometimes did nothing but fan the flames.

There was one call that always came to mind when Luke

responded to a family fight. It was a residence on Peoria Avenue just west of Cave Creek Road. A drunk had knocked his wife around and busted up the kitchen because he didn't like what she'd cooked for supper. Talking to the man proved futile. When he attempted to throw Luke out of the house, the fight was on.

The man was shorter than Luke, but a whole lot heavier. An attempt to apply a choke hold proved futile. The man had no neck. Every time Luke got his arm around the area where his neck should be, he bit Luke in the arm. After a long fight, Luke managed to drag the man outside and subdue him just as his backup arrived. He still had scars on his forearm to remind him about the night he'd tangled with a drunk who was half alligator.

Luke put the thought aside and cautiously approached the frantic man, his hand on his gun.

"What's going on?" he calmly asked.

"She's having a baby. Help her! She's having a baby!" the man yelled.

Luke glanced inside the vehicle. A woman was lying on the back seat, crying and screaming, obviously in labor pains. Her shoes and panties were on the floor and her dress was pulled down between her legs.

Luke quickly returned to his patrol car and notified radio to send an ambulance. He then hurried back to the woman in labor.

His first thought was to tell the woman to keep her legs closed until the ambulance could get there. He quickly dismissed that thought. He had to act now.

"I'm here. You're going to be all right. Just try to follow my directions and everything will be all right," he calmly said.

Who was he trying to convince? Her or himself? Luke couldn't help the thought. But he had to act like he knew what he was doing, even if he was probably just as scared as the woman in labor.

"Relax a little and slow down your breathing," he said.

"Are you nuts?" the woman screamed. "How the hell do you expect me to relax when it feels like my insides are being torn out? Men will never understand. If you were the ones having a baby…Oh, what the hell…Ohhhhh!"

"Yeah. I guess that was kind of a dumb statement." Luke admitted. "I'm going to help you, but I'll need your cooperation. Together we can get through this. Lift your dress and spread your legs as wide as you can. I'll need to see what's going on down there."

Without hesitation, the woman did as directed.

The top of the baby's head was already showing. He resisted the temptation to reach in and grab the head. But giving birth can't be rushed. He'd learned that much from watching animals give birth. He had to wait for the right moment before he'd be able to help. He wished he could have washed his hands first. He wiped them off as best he could on his trousers.

He attempted to talk to the frightened woman in order to calm her down, but most of the time she was screaming and crying too loud to hear.

"Each time you feel a contraction, take a deep breath and push," Luke said.

The woman moaned, screamed, and pushed. There was some dilation, but nothing significant happened.

Maybe he should brace his feet against the woman's butt and pull the baby out, just as he had often helped cattle deliver their babies. He couldn't help but find the thought amusing.

"Push. You're going to have to push harder than that," Luke said

After a few more screams, along with some grunts and groans, the baby's head popped out.

"We're almost done. Push harder," Luke said.

Another blood curdling scream and a long push. The shoulders were out.

Luke gently guided the rest of the baby out, careful to cradle the head. It was a boy.

"Is the baby OK? I don't hear any noise. Is everything OK?" The woman was becoming hysterical as she tried to sit up while reaching for the baby.

Luke cleared the mucous from the baby's mouth and nose and blew in his face. When that didn't cause a stir, he held him by the ankles and smacked him on the butt. Almost immediately, the baby began to cry.

"You have a beautiful baby boy," he said. "He looks healthy too. He sure has a healthy set of lungs."

He laid the baby on the mother's stomach and was trying to find something to wipe his hands on when the ambulance pulled up.

Luke's backup pulled in behind it, but after quickly determining he wasn't needed, hurried off to another call.

Luke watched the medical personnel load the woman and baby into the ambulance and drive away. He needed to find the nearest gas station and wash up. But first he needed to talk with the idiot father.

The man had distanced himself from the commotion in the back seat. He was leaning against the trunk of the patrol car as Luke approached.

Luke wanted to grab the man and shake some sense into him. In fact, he had all he could do to keep from knocking him on his ass.

"What the hell is the matter with you?" he growled. "You know for nine months that your wife is going to have a baby and you wait until the last minute to take her to the hospital? You were just damn lucky it wasn't a breech-birth or the outcome might have been a whole lot different."

"What the hell are you talking about?" the man yelled. "I don't even know that woman. She flagged me down a few blocks away and asked me to take her to the hospital. This is as far as we got. Look at my brand new car. It's ruined. Who's going to pay for cleaning up my car?"

"My apologies," Luke said. "I thought the lady was your wife."

The man gave Luke an angry look and hurried to his car. He was gone by the time Luke finished drying his hands on his handkerchief and his trousers.

Luke suddenly busted out laughing at the mistake he'd made thinking the man who owned the Chrysler was the baby's father. He'd have to be more careful about jumping to conclusions.

He felt good about helping to bring another life into the world. But no good deed goes unpunished. He had to go home and change clothes. Another cleaning bill. Most of the time, it was from rolling around on the ground with a combative suspect, or vomit from a drunk. This time, however, he was a lot more forgiving. He had successfully delivered a baby.

CHAPTER FIFTEEN

"What a mess," Emily groused, while picking up clothing, shoes, and dirty dishes from Becky's room. She wondered why it was that Michael and Amy were neat freaks while Becky was a slob. Like father, like daughter. The thought brought a smile to her face. Luke never seemed to put anything back where it belonged, but he always knew right where everything was. She, on the other hand, kept things neat and orderly, but could never find anything.

Emily straightened out a blanket on the bed that seemed to have a perpetual wrinkle. As she tucked it under the mattress, her hand struck something. She pulled out a plastic bag with a leafy green substance. What was a bag full of leaves doing under the mattress?

She couldn't believe her eyes. What would Becky be doing

with something like that? Maybe it was something for a school project. But that didn't make any sense. No, it must be marijuana. Emily had never seen any in reality, but she had seen pictures and news programs that displayed the stuff.

Her first thought was to call Luke. She stopped short of picking up the phone. Telling him would only put him in a difficult position. He would feel compelled to make a police report, and that would mean Rebecca would have a criminal record. Emily couldn't let that happen. She hurried to the bathroom and dumped the contents in the toilet, flushed, and watched the leafy green material swirl around and disappear. She would have to handle this situation by herself, without involving her husband.

***

Luke arrived home after work to find Becky talking to a young man in the carport. As soon as he pulled in, both walked away.

"Hey, where you going?" he called as he stepped out of his truck. If the young man was his daughter's boyfriend, Luke wanted to meet him.

The couple slowly returned.

"This is Ricky," Rebecca said.

An anxious feeling swept through Luke as he gave Ricky his full attention. Stringy blonde hair and a washed out complexion was indicative of many drug users Luke had arrested. But if he was Becky's friend, he must be OK. She wouldn't have anything to do with a drug user.

"Hi Ricky," Luke said. He offered his hand.

"Hi," the boy replied. He gave Luke's outstretched hand a weak grasp.

"Were you coming or going?" Luke asked while on his way to the door.

"Ricky was just leaving," Becky replied.

"Nice to have met you Ricky," Luke said before stepping inside.

The enticing aroma of fried chicken hit him as soon as he entered. He loved that smell. It reminded him of his childhood days on the farm when his mother would send him out to catch a couple of roosters for supper.

"Something smells awfully good in here." He strolled into the kitchen.

"Supper is almost ready," Emily replied while stirring the gravy. "Did you meet Becky's new boyfriend?"

"Are you serious? That doper-looking guy is Becky's

boyfriend? What the hell is the matter with that girl's head?" Luke hadn't planned on making such negative comments about a friend of his daughter and someone he'd just met, but the words were out before he realized it.

"I met him several weeks ago and tried talking to her. But I'm afraid the more we disapprove, the more she'll insist on seeing him, so I thought it best not to say anything more," Emily said.

She had spoken to Becky about the marijuana under her mattress. Her daughter denied using it. She said she was keeping it at the request of a friend. Emily cautioned her about hanging out with drug users, or being in possession of illegal drugs. She forbid her to ever bring any illegal drugs into the house. Becky agreed not to let it happen again. So Emily would keep the secret, at least for the time being.

"We can't really know what kind of a person he is just by looking at him," Luke said. "I guess we'll have to wait and see what happens. Becky is pretty intelligent–like her mother."

Luke stopped on his way to the coffee pot to give Emily a kiss on the head. "You've often told me what you thought of the way I looked when we first met, and I turned out all right," he chuckled.

"That's debatable," Emily said. She smiled coyly as she put the last dish on the table. "Tell the kids supper is ready."

Luke called Michael and Amy from their rooms and went out to get Becky. She and Ricky were at the end of the driveway.

"Supper's ready," he called.

Ricky hurried away. Becky slowly turned to follow her father into the house.

Luke wanted to grab his daughter and shake some sense into her. He held it in and said nothing as she entered the house and took her usual seat at the table.

After everyone was seated and supper was well underway, Luke asked Becky to tell him something about her boyfriend.

"There's nothing to tell," she said. "He's just a boy I met. We just talk, nothing more."

"Where did you meet?" Luke asked.

"At school."

"He goes to your school?"

"No."

"How did you come to meet at school when he doesn't go to your school?"

"His brother is in my class."

It was obvious to Luke that his daughter resented her father's inquiry and didn't want to discuss her relationship with Ricky.

Luke wanted to find out more, but he didn't want to make

a big deal out of the situation at the dinner table. He would wait for a more appropriate time.

But he was definitely going to find out more about the scruffy looking friend of his daughter. He had a bad feeling about the young man.

***

It was two weeks later that Emily confided to Luke that she had found some marijuana in Becky's room and flushed it down the toilet.

Luke was furious. "Why didn't you tell me sooner? We need to put a stop to this before it gets out of hand. What the hell were you…?"

He stopped himself and managed a weak smile. "You did the right thing. I would have probably made things worse. Sometimes I think you're the one who should be a cop. Your thinking is two steps ahead of mine."

"I told Ricky I'd found marijuana in Becky's room and ordered him to stay away or I'd turn him in to the police. He just laughed it off. He still hangs around," Emily said.

Luke felt his blood pressure shoot up. He forced himself to remain calm. "I'll have a talk with him. Some people take a little more convincing than others."

He didn't know what he was going to do. He never knew what he was going to do until the time came. He just hoped he would do the right thing.

***

The time came for a confrontation with Becky's friend a lot sooner than he anticipated. It was Monday, Luke's day off. The doorbell rang. It was Ricky.

"Is Becky here?" he asked.

"My wife told you to stay away from her," Luke replied before stepping through the door.

"Yeah, well. People tell me a lot of things, but I go where I please."

Before he realized it, Luke had the young man by the throat and up against the side of the house with his feet dangling. "I'm only going to say this once, so listen very carefully. If you ever come around here again, or ever even speak to my daughter again, you will never again speak to anyone else…*ever again.* The desert is a big place. They will never find your body. Do you believe me? Do I make myself clear?" He lowered the boy to the ground.

The color had drained from the boy's face. He stood with head bowed.

"Yes sir," he meekly said. He shuffled out to the sidewalk and down the street, away from the school.

Luke watched him go. He knew he could get into a lot of trouble for grabbing the young man and threatening his life, but when it came to his family, legality be damned.

He realized he might have to deal with Rebecca's resentment for chasing away her boyfriend. But that was little price to pay for keeping her away from illegal drugs and those who use them.

During the months that followed, however, Becky didn't seem upset. She eventually revealed to her parents that Ricky had been arrested at the Mexican border trying to smuggle heroin into the country.

CHAPTER SIXTEEN

All uniformed patrol officers still rotated shifts every two months, and each time night shift rolled around, Luke went through the same routine with Emily.

It was 9 p.m. when he started getting ready for work. His shift didn't start until ten, but he always left early. He was careful never to be late for work. He held his subordinates to the same standard.

All the while Luke was getting dressed, Emily was pleading with him not to go.

"You were just on nights. Why do you have to go back so soon? I thought you only changed shifts every two months? Can't you switch with someone who wants to work nights?"

"No, I can't switch with anyone. It's been four months

since I worked nights. It's time to do it again," Luke explained.

"I hate it when you work nights," Emily said. "I don't like sleeping alone. I always feel better when I can reach over and touch you. I never sleep well when you aren't there."

"I don't like it either," Luke said. He put his arms around her and held her close. "It'll be over before you know it," he whispered in her ear. "Besides, you have three kids and a dog to keep you company. That's a pretty good trade for one used husband, don't you think?"

"Sometimes, I'd trade the lot of you for one man who'd stay home with me at night," Emily said. She gave Luke a quick kiss and nudged him to the door. "You'd better get going or they'll make you work an extra month of nights for being late. Be careful out there," she added.

He had already made the rounds of each child's bedroom before getting dressed. Each was catching up on homework and didn't seem as interested in a prolonged goodbye as they once were. Luke gave them a quick kiss on the head and left them to continue with their work.

He pulled his jacket tightly around him and shivered as he got into his truck. It was a relief to work nights in the summer and escape the relentless heat. But in the winter, it got downright cold.

***

It was the middle of January and closing in on 2 a.m. Saturday morning when Luke received a radio call from one of his officers to see him at a west Phoenix residence.

He rolled up to the curb to find a group of people milling about in the driveway.

As soon as he came to a stop, Officer Jimmy Foster was there to greet him. Foster fit the mold of a typical Phoenix police officer: tall, lean and sinewy, spit-shined shoes and pressed uniform, his hat positioned perfectly straight on his head.

"Hi Sarge," Foster said. He glanced back and forth between his sergeant and the group by the house. "Thanks for coming so quickly. I wasn't sure what to do about this situation. I've never had anything like it before."

"No problem. That's what I get the big bucks for." Luke grabbed his flashlight and stepped out of the car. "What's going on?"

"Well," Foster continued, "the man who lived here recently died, leaving behind his son and his wife who is the child's stepmother. The father was granted custody of the baby at the time of divorce and had since remarried. The boy is now a little over a year old."

Foster nervously continued to exchange glances between the people in front of the house and his sergeant while continuing to explain the situation. "The dead man's ex-wife and birth mother of the child lives out of state. She's here to claim her son. In his will, however, the father said he wanted his present wife, the child's stepmother, to have custody of the child. But now, the birth mother, her new husband, their attorney and other relatives are here to get the baby. They demand the stepmother hand over the child, but the stepmother refuses to let them in, and she refuses to hand over the baby."

Foster pointed out two men arguing toe to toe. Their angry voices easily reached beyond the yard where they stood.

"Those two men are attorneys. Each side has an attorney representing them, and each is demanding custody of the child. But neither one is able to show a legal document that supports their claim. The only thing anyone has in writing is a copy of the will in which the father willed custody of the child to the stepmother."

"Any attorney should know you can't *will* people," Luke said. He glanced at the two groups–one huddled on the lawn and the other in the driveway–before turning his attention back to Officer Foster.

"Have you physically checked the child to see if he's all right, and see what the living conditions are inside?" Luke asked.

"No, I've just been out here trying to keep the peace between the two sides. I didn't want a big fight to start. So far, they've all been pretty vocal, but they've pretty much kept their distance from each other except for the attorneys. I just let them continue to yell at each other. It kept them busy. I thought I had better just stay out here and keep the peace until you got here," Foster followed his sergeant up the drive.

"Good thinking," Luke said.

Attorneys Roger Graves and Julian Wax came to meet the sergeant; each trying to shout down the other and tell their side first.

"I'm Sergeant Canfield," he told them. "I'll have to ask you to keep your voices down. The neighbors are obviously asleep and we don't want a *disturbing the peace* complaint from one of them. I'm going inside to check the welfare of the child. Then I'll come back and see if we can get this situation ironed out. Just give me a minute."

He knocked on the door and identified himself. The stepmother, Bessie Milton, slowly opened the door.

She was a frail woman, five-foot-five maybe, and about ninety pounds. Her long brown hair hung over the shoulders of a blue cotton bathrobe wrapped tightly around her slender body.

"I have sole custody," she said. She slowly backed away so the sergeant could enter the house. "My husband requested in his will that I retain custody of our son."

"We'll sort all that out later," Luke replied as he walked into the room. "Right now, I'd like to see the child. I need to know that he's all right."

Bessie led the way to a back bedroom. As Luke followed, he glanced around the house. Everything was clean and orderly. *Nice furniture, clean floors, elegant curtains. I wouldn't mind being raised here myself.*

He tiptoed into the bedroom where the baby was sleeping and was immediately met with the familiar aroma of baby powder and oil. *Smells like a baby's room should.*

Luke glanced at the small figure sleeping peacefully in the large crib. He thought of his own children and all of the work it took for two people to raise them properly.

It has got to be twice as hard for only one parent.

His attention drifted back and forth between the stepmother and the child.

"I don't want to disturb his sleep, but I need to examine his body to make sure everything is all right," he whispered. He began to remove the blanket from the sleeping child.

"I'll do it," Bessie said. She slowly reached across Luke's arm and lifted the blanket.

"That's probably a better idea," Luke said. He moved his arm to make room for the stepmother. "I'm sure you're more adept at it than me. I don't want to wake him, but I'm sure you understand. I need to see that the baby is OK before we go any further."

Bessie remained silent as she continued to slowly remove the blanket as if unwrapping a delicate piece of crystal.

Luke examined the baby and found him to be in good physical condition. He smelled clean, like babies should. Powder and oil was the only aroma.

"It looks like you've been an excellent mother," Luke said.

They left the bedroom and headed down the hall. "Thanks for your patience. I'll go talk with the birth mother and her attorney."

Bessie's tired eyes shot him a disgusted, and at the same time, a frightened look. "As well as your attorney," he hurriedly added, "and see if we can get something worked out that's agreeable to both sides."

She must know she's going to have to give him up. The thought came to Luke as he prepared to leave the house. *I don't blame her for being disgusted and frightened, especially after caring for the baby for the past year.*

The two people stood silently by the front door; a mother and a police sergeant. Both realized a decision must be made. And one of them was terrified of being the loser.

The widow had undoubtedly been attractive at one time. Luke couldn't help the thought. But that was before the repo man arrived in the guise of an attorney. He was there to take back her happiness. Her lease was up. She must return the bundle of joy. But she wasn't giving him up without a fight.

Bessie touched Luke's arm. Not so much to prevent the inevitable, but merely to postpone it. Luke had planned a quick look inside and a quicker exit so he wouldn't get caught up in taking sides. But this woman had disrupted his plans. The more he was in her presence, the more he understood what she was feeling. He could see the drops of liquid slowly forming in the corners of her sad brown eyes. She choked back the tears that would continue to build until, fueled by gravity, they would come bounding down her face.

Her trembling lips uttered a final plea. "I was never able to give birth to a child," Bessie said in little more than a whisper, "so God blessed me with this one. I've raised him since he was three months old. I couldn't feel more like his mother if he was my flesh and blood. If he is taken from me, my heart will go with him."

Luke was filled with empathy for the fragile figure in front of him. She looked even smaller with her hunched shoulders and dangling sleeves of the oversized robe. Unruly strands of hair hung down along the outside corners of her eyes. They appeared to act as symbolic quotation marks that framed the heart-wrenching story that her face was telling.

He fought to resist putting his arms around her and telling her not to cry. That wouldn't do. It wouldn't be appropriate. So he stood there, feeling her silent pleading not to take a part of her that she had already given away.

In Luke's mind, Bessie was more of a mother than many who had given birth, and she was doing everything in her power to protect her child. That's what mothers are supposed to do. They divide their heart into pieces—one portion for each child. Some children treasure the gift. Others stash theirs in the junk-drawer of their mind, forgotten and mingled with other items they seldom use. While others simply throw theirs away.

This trembling soul standing by the door had given her entire heart to one child. Now someone has come to claim it. A robbery was being committed, and Sergeant Luke Canfield, the bastion of public safety, was a reluctant accomplice.

Bessie's hand dropped from his arm as he turned to leave. He knew he couldn't change the final outcome. But he could buy her a little more time.

He slowly opened the door and stepped out to face the angry relatives and the two attorneys who were impatiently waiting for his decision. Each demanded the sergeant agree with their interpretation of who had rights to the child.

"I checked the child and he appears to be in excellent physical condition," Luke said as he glanced from one attorney to the other. "I also checked the house. It's clean and well kept. I'm sure we all agree that the welfare of the child comes first."

Both attorneys continued to stare at the sergeant without speaking.

"That being the case, here is the decision I've made," he continued. "There appears to be no good reason for taking this baby out of the house at this hour of the night. It is cold out here and the child is sleeping. My first concern, which I'm sure is your concern as well, is what is best for the child. So, he will stay where he is for the time being. On Monday, I suggest that you both go to the court and secure a legal decision as to who gets custody. It is common knowledge that you can't will people, but for right now, the child stays where he is."

Luke no more than got the words out of his mouth than the birth mother stepped up.

"That is my child and we are not leaving here without

him," she angrily exploded. "Either she brings him out or we're going in and get him." She started to the door.

"That is not an acceptable decision," her attorney added. "We demand that you hand over the child without further delay."

"So you're interpreting the law now too?" the other attorney questioned as he angrily confronted Sergeant Canfield. "You're a cop, not a judge," he added. "I want the name of your supervisor."

"I do too," the other attorney said as he pulled out pen and paper and prepared to write down the information.

In anticipation of negative reaction to his decision, Luke maintained his position in front of the door.

"Hold on a minute. If neither of you are in agreement with my decision, there's another alternative. I'll let both sides decide which way you want to go with this. Either we leave the child where he is, asleep and safe in a nice warm bed, or I call Child Welfare. They'll come and get the child and put him in a foster home until the legal custody situation gets ironed out. Of course, they probably won't take him out until the morning. Once the child is fostered out, it will probably take several weeks, or even months, before the case winds itself through the courts. Do either of you want to wait that long for a resolution, when it could be resolved in a day or two?"

He hesitated for a few seconds before continuing, his voice taking on a steely tone that was honed through years of forcing people to obey.

"Let me add one more thing. If anyone attempts to force their way into this house, they will be arrested. I want to make myself clear on that. Anyone will be arrested."

Luke glanced from the attorneys to their clients and back again. No one was saying anything. Each was silent. The two men who were so vocal a few minutes earlier, acted as if their mouths were glued shut. For the first time in Luke's career, he was in the presence of an attorney who was at a loss for words. Not only that, but there were two of them—and both remained silent.

"Well, which is it to be? Either the child stays where he is for now or he goes to foster care. It's your choice, but I think we've been out here long enough."

Both sides reluctantly accepted Luke's unpopular decision. He provided the name of his supervisor and waited until the two attorneys and their entourage, still arguing with each other, climbed into their cars and drove away. The manicured lawn of Bessie Milton was once more a calm and peaceful landscape.

"Thanks, Sarge. I'm sure glad you showed up. Frankly, I wouldn't have known what to tell them." Foster followed his sergeant to his car.

"No problem," Luke responded. "In situations like this, you usually can't go wrong by maintaining the status quo. Just remember to first do no harm. I'm sure the birth mother will get custody. That's just common sense. But our first consideration is always for the most vulnerable. In this case, it's the child."

Luke hurried to find the nearest pay phone. He always kept his boss informed, and he wanted to tell him about this latest incident and the decision he'd made before the attorneys called.

After hearing Luke's explanation, Lieutenant Harvy agreed he'd made the right call.

The following night, as Luke was finishing up his paperwork before going on patrol, Lieutenant Harvy called him into his office.

What now? Are those two attorneys still complaining? Luke couldn't help the thought as he made his way down the hall.

He entered the lieutenant's office and stood in front of his desk. Harvy was always so militaristic, Luke felt like snapping to attention and saying, "Sergeant Canfield reporting as ordered, Sir."

Instead, he remained silent, waiting for what his lieutenant had to say.

"Have a seat," Lieutenant Harvy said, while still focusing on a report he was holding.

Luke didn't like that. He was always wary when his boss told him to have a seat. That meant a longer period of time for a lecture or lengthy directive. Luke didn't like to linger in the station. He always felt better when he was out following up on calls. He had a lot of new guys out there.

He breathed a sigh of resignation and settled into the chair that was situated perfectly in line with the Lieutenant's gaze.

After a few minutes of silence, Harvy gave Luke his full attention. It always reminded Luke of the same thoroughness with which a surgeon eyes a patient before inserting the scalpel.

"Have you ever considered working administration?" Harvy asked, his voice trailing away as his attention was diverted momentarily to the desk aide bringing in some papers.

The question caught Luke by surprise. "No, never," he quickly answered.

Harvy set the papers aside and once more gave Luke his undivided attention.

"I've been impressed with the quality and timeliness of your reports," Harvy said. "You have also exercised good judgment on several occasions."

Luke didn't know what to say about that. His boss seldom complemented anyone on anything. Why is he doing it now? What was he getting at?

The lieutenant quit talking. Luke didn't know if he was expected to respond or just keep his mouth shut. He couldn't stand the suspense any longer.

"Thanks," Luke said, "I do the paperwork because I have to, not because I like to. In my opinion, there's way too much of it. I should be out on the street with my troops instead of spending so much time on paperwork."

"I'm just trying to figure out why no one has tapped you for their administrative sergeant," Harvy said. He again focused his attention on some papers he was holding.

It was sometimes difficult to tell when he was dismissed, even when the eyes quit their steady gaze. Luke remained seated. Not only because he wasn't sure if Harvy was done talking, but because his mind was racing to find the reason for the conversation. After a few tense minutes, the lieutenant looked up.

"That's all I wanted to talk with you about," he said.

Luke got up and headed for the door. He couldn't get out of there fast enough. Administration? Why the hell is he asking me about administration? He shuddered at the thought.

CHAPTER SEVENTEEN

On Tuesday of the following week, the answer to Luke's question of why he was being queried about administration hit him right between the eyes. Among the paperwork in his in-box was a transfer memo with his name on it. Lieutenant Harvy was being promoted to Captain and assigned to the main station. He was taking Luke along as his administrative sergeant.

Luke read it and reread it, trying to find an error, a loophole of some kind that would render the transfer void. Try as he might, he couldn't find one. With paper in hand, he hurried to Lieutenant Harvy's office.

"I appreciate the consideration," Luke told the soon-to-be captain, "but I don't want to work administration. I belong in the field. I'm sure there are a lot of competent sergeants who would love to go, but I'm not one of them."

A slow smile crossed Harvy's face as he watched his sergeant, who was so calm and controlled on the street, squirm like a worm on a hook.

"I don't know anything about administration," Luke continued. "I can best serve the department by remaining in the field."

The smile disappeared from Harvy's lips. A carefully measured tone took its place.

"You know as well as I that a good administrative sergeant is hard to find," he said. "You're as good as I've seen. I trust you and I want you as my admin sergeant. Wind things up with your squad and make sure everything is ready for your replacement. Your transfer is effective Monday."

Luke stood silently for a few minutes. He wanted to try and convince his lieutenant that he'd made the wrong choice. But he knew from past experience, once Lieutenant Harvy made up his mind, he wasn't going to change it.

During his drive home that morning, Luke's mind was filled with thoughts of what he could have said or should have done.

I know one person who's going to be happy with this transfer. The thought came to him as he quietly entered the house.

Skippy was his only greeter, and he lingered only long enough for a sniff and a wag of his tail before resuming his usual position sprawled out on the floor.

After washing up, Luke tried not to wake his wife as he crept silently into bed. This was the best part of the day. It was worth working nights if he could come home while it was still dark and snuggle up against his wife before she had to get up and see the kids off to school. He eased over to feel her warm body without disturbing her sleep.

"I'm glad you're home," she whispered.

"I tried not to wake you," he replied. "But since you're awake, I'll tell you I won't be working nights any longer. I'm being transferred to administration Monday, so I'll be working days from now on."

"That's worth waking up for," Emily whispered. She turned to face him and buried her face in his neck. "That's the best thing you could have said, other than you love me."

"I love you," Luke replied as their bodies melded together.

"Maybe administration isn't going to be so bad after all," he mused as Emily pulled his body on top of hers and wrapped her long legs around him.

The warmth of her supple body and the fragrance of her lingering perfume created a euphoria that permeated every cell of

Luke's being. Forgotten were the shattered dreams of youth, the burdensome thoughts of past mistakes and those yet to come. In the back of his mind, he knew it was only a temporary reprieve. He would pick those emotional burdens up again when he left for work. But for now, everything was as it should be. His children were safely asleep in their beds and he was wrapped in the arms of his loving wife. Life was good.

The End

Made in the USA
San Bernardino, CA
16 June 2019